A SECOND CHANCE
VOLUME 3
BY EDMOND WHITE

Table of Contents

Table of Contents

Chapter 28

Paul

I have to find a way to contact Sheila without being spotted. She can tend to my dislocated arm. I pace through the city, heading for Yale New Haven Hospital. It's been five months since I've been outside the asylum. The city feels the same. A block ahead, I spot two beat cops heading in my direction.

I blend in with the crowd, walking on the sidewalk, careful not to draw attention to myself. I act normal and even nod at the officers, acknowledging them. They politely return the gesture and continue on their beat. A block away from the hospital, I stop inside a Dunkin Doughnuts. I have to find a phone to call my sister. I sit at the table, scanning the room for anyone with a cell phone. The line in front of the counter extends to the door as people buy coffee before work. I contemplate asking someone waiting at the end of the line who has a longer wait instead of someone on their way out. The bar is composed of primarily white women. From my seat, I try to detect the polite ones near the end of the line. I spot a friendly face. She has just finished talking on her phone.

"Excuse me, miss, I lost my cell phone. I need to call my wife. It's sort of an emergency. Can I use your phone for a few minutes?" The elderly Caucasian woman inspects me up and down before halfheartedly handing over her phone. I dialed my sister's number. She answers.

"Hello?"

"Sharon, it's me, Paul."

"Paul, I can't talk right now. I'm working."

"Sharon, it's an emergency. I need your help," the line of mostly women turn to face me. I lower my voice.

"What kind of emergency?"

"I need you to pick me up."

"From the asylum?"

"No, from the Dunkin Doughnuts down the street."

"What are you doing in a Dunkin' Donuts?"

"It's a long story, and I have a broken arm. Can you get something from the hospital to ease the pain? I'll explain the rest when you pick me up."

"Today isn't a good day, Paul. I have a lot of patients to attend to. I can't just walk out on them," she says nothing for a few seconds. The Caucasian woman in line is getting her coffee.

"Sharon, please. I cover my mouth. They're framing me for murder."

"Murder? Ok, I'm leaving now," within minutes, her silver Dodge Durango pulls up in front of the Dunkin Donuts. I get inside her truck.

"Paul, what's going on? And how did you get here?" I tell her the entire story when she pulls away from the Dunkin Doughnuts. After I finished explaining the details to her, she was mystified.

"What will you do, Paul? They will eventually find you."

"I didn't kill Alexandria."

"I believe you, Paul, but Bedford is a mental institution. Do you think the police will believe your words over a psychiatrist?"

"Why wouldn't they? I'm a pastor of a church. My word is honest."

"You were a church pastor. When they arrested you, that title ended. They don't see you as a pastor anymore. Most people see you as a crazed individual."

"I'm not a lunatic, Sharon. I'm perfectly sane and have the evidence to back it up."

"Who killed Alexandria then?"

"I'm not sure, but I have a hunch. When the doctor and I climbed out of the chamber, I saw a hole cut in the fence behind us. The person probably entered the chamber and went upstairs to the rooms. The doctor said my belongings were near Alexandria's body, and my room door was the only one open on the floor."

"So you think someone did this to frame you?" Her eyes widen.

"I do."

"Who would break into an asylum to do this?"

"Patricia."

"It doesn't make sense, Paul. Why would she go through all this trouble?"

"To put me away permanently, I'm sure of it. Who else could have this type of hatred towards me?"

"You believe she would kill an innocent woman to frame you? Then why did it take her five months and not sooner?"

"She had to plan it out, Sharon. It took time."

"If that's the case, we need to find some answers as to why. In the meantime, you must stay out of sight until we find the truth. The police will be searching the entire state, looking for you. I know a place where you can stay. The police will never look for you there."

"Where?"

"My boyfriend's apartment."

"I'm not comfortable with this idea."

"Paul, do you have any other choice?"

"I guess not."

"You'll be fine," she's right. I don't have anywhere to go.

"Does he know about me?"

"I haven't spoken about you."

"What type of job does he have?"

"Take a lucky guess," she smiles.

"A minister?"

"Yes. I've been surrounded by ministers all my life. He's a good man. You will feel right at home. He's serving as an assistant pastor at a local church," I guess she's keeping it in the family. We arrive at her boyfriend's pad in no time. He's very hospitable and seems to be fond of my sister. When Sharon explained my situation to him, he waited until she finished before commenting.

"Would you like something to drink, Paul?"

"Water is fine."

"I don't mind helping you out. God tells us to help those in need and not judge. I know this must be a difficult time for you. This woman, where did you meet her?" He asks, getting a bottle of water out of the fridge.

"I met her at a church retreat. She told me a friend of hers recommended she hear me preach. She said she was moved after hearing one of my sermons and decided to become a church member," Sharon's boyfriend mulls it over momentarily.

"Have you ever met her family?" The question was simple. In most normal relationships, one usually meets the family of the significant other after dating for some time. When I dated Patricia, I never met anyone in her family. The question was sort of baffling to me. His dark profile probes over me. He raises an eyebrow.

"I haven't. To be honest, I don't know much about Patricia. I was too fixated on her to learn more about her family."

"It happens to us all when we're in love," he smiles at my sister, and she returns the gesture.

"Well, little brother, we need to find her parents. Her parents may help answer some of our questions."

"Sharon, I'm on it. I will look for her mother. She has to know something."

After getting some much-needed rest, I awake with determination. Brendon slept on the couch last night, allowing me the comfort of his king-sized bed. Sharon has found a winner. I wish them the best. He gives me access to his computer before leaving for work. I started my search. I typed in Columbia University, where Patricia graduated from. The name Patricia Martin doesn't appear in any yearbook I look through online. It is probably a lie. My guess is she never attended

Columbia University. I click through pages and pages of graduates and find nothing. I'm mentally exhausted from the search. I shut down the computer and try to relax while my mind is still forming questions. Is Patricia her real name? Where did she come from? Why is she trying to destroy me? It's now noon time, and I'm famished. Brandon's refrigerator has meats, leafy greens, and dairy products. I take two slices of wheat bread from the loaf on his kitchen counter.

After spreading mayonnaise on the two slices, I place a portion of turkey breast and Swiss cheese between the bread. I grab a bottle of water and sit in front of Brandon's fifty-five-inch screen.

I'm curious if the cops are combing the streets for me. I turn to channel seven, and there she is. Anchorwoman Danita Stokes is reporting another story. How convenient is it to have the leverage to make or break a person's life? She is the most popular news anchorwoman in the state. When she reports, people tend to listen, especially African Americans. Her stories fill the dinner tables, barber shops, grocery stores, and wherever people gather. Most people take her word for granted. If Danita wrote it, then it must be true. She has a considerable following. Many believe she will one day have success, similar to Oprah Winfrey.

When charged with raping Patricia, Danita made it her business to interview me. I would've probably gone to jail right after my arrest, but the state considered me to be mentally incompetent to stand trial at the time of the accusation. The state sent me to Bedford Mental Institution instead. During the interview, she asked me why I raped Patricia. I told her I never put my hands on Patricia. Her interrogation appeared worse than a detective's. She harassed me for the truth. I advised her to leave me when I couldn't take it anymore. That's when I saw the other side of her. She made ample threats, and her approach puzzled me. Danita promised she would bring me down to the lowest level possible, and I would never be able to preach again. She told me she detested rapists more than anything on earth. Watching her on television, I feel the hairs on my neck.

Chapter 29

China

China is sitting up in the hospital bed. The doctor performed a thorough examination of her body, and no broken bones were present or internal bleeding. He informed China and Mark he needed to run additional tests for any sexually transmitted diseases. If everything clears, he tells China she is free to leave. Two NHPD detectives are standing outside her door, waiting to question her about the rape.

"Honey, are you still upset with me?"

"China, I'm not upset with you," Mark replies.

"Then why did you act that way inside the truck?" He walks over to the bed.

"The two of you gave me every reason to act like that. At first, I tried to ignore it."

"Ignore what? I don't understand."

"The way the two of you act around each other. He is always near you, and you seem to enjoy every minute of laughing, giggling, and whispering to each other. I've seen the two of you blowing kisses on a few occasions. I know you needed him for security, but it never felt right to me at all. I hate the subtle innuendos. The two of you are constantly doing things that make you look like a couple," she reaches for Mark's hand. He reluctantly takes hers.

"A couple? Mark, he worked for me? We developed a platonic relationship over the years, nothing more."

"Then, why does he prioritize pulling you away from me every time you and I are together?"

"How?"

"Something always comes up, that's how."

"Mark, I'm a celebrity. Events, appearances, performances, it's what I do. You can't blame him for that. It's part of my job."

"I'm not talking about that part of your job. The part I'm referring to has nothing to do with that. It's all Jason's doing. It's like he knows when we have something planned. He interrupted our plans more than once. Do you remember when I flew out to stay with you a few years back?"

"Yes, you were on vacation."

"We planned to stay indoors for the day and have fun with each other. Your chef had prepared a great dish, and we both agreed to walk around the mansion nude, playing enticing games after dinner. And then he shows up claiming you weren't safe. He said he received a letter from a crazed fan, and he might attempt to show up at your door with all the security you had outside. Did that make any kind of sense to you?"

"Mark, you don't know how many threats I've received from fans over the years. Some of these individuals will try and do anything to get near me. It made perfect sense."

"Ok, I'll give you that one. But what about when you and I wanted to see a movie at one of the local theaters?"

"I don't recall that. Refresh my memory," China touches the bandage on her forehead.

"China, you said you wanted to go to a movie theater and watch a movie like a normal person without people coming up to you."

"I remember."

"You put on a slight disguise and lowered yourself in the back of my truck as I made my way through the gate. We eventually made it to the theater, enjoying the movie. Then, he taps our shoulders from the seat behind us and asks us if we want popcorn," she laughs.

"Oh, this is funny to you?"

"It was at the time. I wanted popcorn, but I didn't want to risk getting noticed. And as soon as you decided to get us some, Jason showed up with two bags."

"I'm glad you find this amusing. The man raped you, and you're laughing at his antics," his comment offends China.

"Mark, I think you should leave the room. I want to be left alone."

"I'm sorry, China, for bringing up the rape again."

"Just leave Mark. I need to clear my head."

"Honestly, I'm sorry," she turns away from him. He departs.

Mark remains unsure of where their relationship is heading. He firmly believes Jason is more than just her employee. China's placid body language makes him suspect something is going on. His intuition is telling him she gave into Jason perhaps additional times. Mark sits outside the room where the detectives wait patiently to question her. The officers glare at him, and he reciprocates the favor. Back inside the room, China cannot escape her feelings. She closes her eyes to clear her head, but Jason's silhouette appears each time she shuts them. Although he raped and took advantage of her, she desires to be near him. Initially, she clawed and fought desperately to scratch her way to freedom. She even managed to slap him, which provoked him to strike her across the forehead. But then, instead of things turning for the worse, it became exotic and passionate. She gave into his adoring kisses, his soft caresses, and his climatic strokes. Again and again, he plunges inside of her, unlocking her hidden inhibitions. When Jason finishes exploring her body, the two of them stare at each other in utter silence. Jason has poured himself into her—the years of wanting her and waiting patiently to have her have finally come to fruition for Jason. China refuses to tell Mark how she truly feels. He loves her, and China loves him. How can she forget about Jason? Pressing charges against Jason will put him away and end their love affair. She needs to see him again and rekindle the moment in her bedroom. Never before has a man ignited her body entirely. Mark is an excellent lover, but nothing compared to Jason. China takes several strands of her hair and brings them closer to her nose. She inhales profoundly, savoring Jason's scent. A knock on the door interrupts her fantasy.

"Come in," she says politely. Two NHPD detectives walk inside the room. The taller of the two speaks first.

"Ms. Reynolds, first, I would like to say I love your music. My daughter is an avid fan of yours. I promised her I would get your autograph upon questioning you. That's if it's ok with you," the shorter detective shakes his head.

"She's not feeling well," he whispers. "How can you ask for her autograph at a time like this?"

"I'm quite alright," China interjects. "I haven't signed an autograph in some time. It would be a pleasure too," the taller detective gives the shorter one a staid look. China signs the front of his daughter's poster of her. The more diminutive detective starts the questioning.

"Ms. Reynolds, can you explain to us what happened on the night you were raped?"

"I would prefer it if you called me China. Ms. Reynolds sounds like an old lady to me. I haven't reached that status yet." "Ok, China." the short, stout detective with the beady eyes agrees. "My bodyguard didn't rape me," the detectives stare at each other.

Chapter 30
David,

Exactly two floors below China, is where the doctors operate on David. After several hours of attempting to remove the bullet lodged in his skull, the doctors decided to terminate the surgery. Taking essential precautions to protect his brain, the doctors forewarned David that any further attempts to remove the bullet may cause severe brain damage. A bandage covers David's head. He is somewhat groggy after the unsuccessful surgery. Touching the mummy wrap around his forehead in dismay, he cannot believe he's alive. He remembers so vividly pressing the gun against his temple and squeezing the trigger. How is it that he's still breathing? Why had the bullet stopped? Logic told him he should be dead. He never attended a church service, read a bible, or knelt to pray. And for good measure, he assumes. What good has it done for so many to pray and worship to a make-believe God for all their lives? What have they gained from their undying faith? Nothing is what David tells himself, absolutely nothing. His hospital room is quiet. David assumes he's the only patient in his room. He likes it that way; no one bothers him. Then, he hears a noise stirring in the corner. Someone is there with him.

"Who's there?"

"It's me, David."

"Nate?"

"I don't know how many times I told mom to get rid of that gun. I knew something awful would happen one day," he says, smirking.

"It's not her fault, Nate. The blame belongs to me."

"If the gun hadn't been there, you wouldn't be in the hospital right now."

"I probably would've found another way to do it, trust me."

"I'm confused, David. You have so much, while others have so little. Why do you want to kill yourself?" David presses the up arrow on the remote control as the bed inclines. Nate leaves his seat to help prop him up.

"To live like this is hard. I don't want anyone to have sympathy for me. I've always done everything by myself. I'm a man, Nate. Wealth, status, and fame mean nothing to me without my sight. I would give it all up to see again," his words are heavy laden with pain. Nate refuses to let the words impact his heart. As far as he's concerned, David is a dead man walking.

"David, I don't know if I could ever take my life no matter what was happening to me."

"I felt the same way at first. I guess we all do until something catastrophic happens to us. Everyone has a breaking point."

"How does your head feel?"

"Surprisingly, I don't feel a thing. The doctor said the bullet is in a section of my brain that regulates pain. He said I could cut or burn myself and not even feel it until it was too late. I have to be careful not to injure myself," Nate's information is getting better by the minute.

"You can't feel anything?"

"Not really; it's like a numbing sensation throughout my body. Let me show you what I mean. I want you to dig your nails into my skin."

"I get it, David. I'd rather not."

"No, it's alright. Don't worry, I won't feel it," Nate digs his nails deep into David's forearm."

"Nate, you can start anytime now."

"My fingernails are already pressed into your skin. My nails aren't that long, but you should feel something."

"I don't feel a thing."

"Tell me something, will they ever be able to remove the bullet?"

"Honestly, I don't think so. Removing it may cause permanent brain damage. The doctors are refusing to take that risk."

"Can't you get a second opinion?" He tries to sound more concerned.

"I can try, but it will probably be a long shot. Maybe Keisha can find some other doctors."

"I'm afraid that might not happen."

"Why?"

"The police have her in custody. David, the gun that fired to kill yourself with was in a street homicide."

"That's impossible. The gun belonged to Uncle Chuck. He had a permit for it."

"I thought the same thing, David. Remember the thirty-eight special?"

"Yes, how could I forget?"

"Well, apparently, Chuck wanted more firepower and purchased the 9mm from a street dealer."

"Are you kidding me? Uncle Chuck would never buy a gun from a street dealer. He hated street thugs," Nate grits his teeth.

"Well, someone put it there."

"So you think your mother put it there?"

"I'm just saying it was either her or Chuck."

"How long can the police hold her?"

"Until they find out more about the gun, she will probably need a lawyer."

"When you contact your mother, tell her I know a few good lawyers that can help her. It isn't her fault. I should receive the blame."

"In the meantime, what will you do?"

"I can't say for sure. I know living alone is out of the question. Not after what I tried to do to myself," Cathy clears her voice.

"You will not be alone. I'm here," startled, Nate turns around. The woman standing in the doorway is a sheer, unblemished beauty from head to toe. She is wearing tight-fitted blue jeans and a navy blue sweater. Nate loses his composure and has to turn away from her.

"Cathy, you didn't have to come. I'm managing just fine. I don't want to hear any scripture. I just need time to think."

"I didn't come this long way to preach. I came to support you and to give you a hand. Will you accept my help?" A couple of male nurses stand behind her, admiring her figure from the entranceway.

"Why do you want to help me?"

"David, you need help. What kind of person would I be if I just sat back and allowed you to struggle alone? I'm not heartless, David. I know the last time we saw each other didn't go well. I'm here to lend a hand the best way I can. I won't preach to you," David has thought about her for some time. He misses her company. If she will support him and keep her Christian experiences to herself, David doesn't mind if she stays. He recalls how magnificent she looks. His displeasure sets in from not being able to see Cathy's appearance. Even though he's unable to see her, the sound of her voice lightens his mood.

"Hi, I'm Cathy," she walks over and extends her hand to Nate.

"Hi, I'm Nate. I'm David's stepbrother," he shakes her hand, lowering his gaze.

"You know, I thought long and hard about the last time we were together, David. It was pretty much my doing the way we split up. I shouldn't have said what I said. I had no right to judge you. I'm no different than you are. Sometimes, I get carried away when I talk about the lord. I realize he comes to us all at different times."

"Cathy, you're doing it again."

"Excuse me, I will change the subject," she smiles.

"I appreciate it, thanks."

"David, I'll see you later. You guys need some privacy."

"OK, don't forget to tell Keisha about the lawyers."

"I won't."

"I didn't know you had a stepbrother?"

"Well, my uncle married his mother."

"Are you two very close?"

"We used to be. As children, we did everything together. We attended the same high school and hung out with similar friends. When I dated one of his girlfriends, it tore us apart," her eyes widen.

"You dated one of his girlfriends? You're a bad boy," she teases.

"I dated her before he even met her."

"Why did this upset him?"

"I don't know," Cathy isn't buying it.

"Yes, you do. You don't sound too convincing."

"Nate didn't receive the same attention as I did when meeting girls. He was sort of shy growing up. I taught him to be confident and socialize more with his peers. Everywhere I went, I made sure he came with me. He learned how to open up more by watching me. There was only one problem."

"What kind of problem?"

"Whenever girls approached us, they always wanted me. I tried to push them onto Nate, but they were never interested in him."

"You're handsome, David. Who wouldn't want you?"

"Cathy, please stop it. I bet I don't look handsome now?" She thoroughly looks him over.

"The bandages are kind of sexy. It works for you."

"Will you please be quiet?" She laughs again.

"Can I finish the story about Nate?"

"Don't mind me. Go right ahead."

"You're something else, woman. As I said before rudely interrupted, Nate felt unwanted. His insecurities started to creep in more and more. To counter this, I avoided him when women came near us. He was very fond of this one girl. He even brought her over to meet his mother. I had football practice that day. I was returning home when they were heading out of the house. Once I saw her face, I knew Nate would find out. I dated his new girlfriend for two months before he met her. I think it hurt our relationship."

"He seemed kind of upset when I came in the room."

"Upset?"

"He didn't look happy, like something was bothering him."

"I don't think he would hold a grudge this long. Uncle Chuck's death probably saddens him, and then seeing me in this condition."

"I don't know David. There was some built-up tension going on."

"I'm sure he's ok. He's been here to support me, and I appreciate it."

"Yes, he has. Maybe I'm exaggerating things a bit."

"How was your trip, Cathy?"

"Safe, the way these planes are going down. Getting here in one piece is a great flight. The plane trip did not match the mob in front of the hospital."

"What are you talking about?"

"There's a camera crew outside. I could barely make it through the doors with all of the spectators. Have you heard anything?"

"I haven't heard anything. Cathy, turn on the TV; maybe it's a live broadcast."

Chapter 31
Paul

Danita Stokes is slinging dirt as usual. She is probably padding her resume for bigger and better things to come. China Reynolds's rape is not a secret anymore, or is David Parks attempted suicide. Part of the world knows, and more will discover when the day ends. If she knew I escaped from the asylum, she would drop both stories in a heartbeat and pursue me like a thirsty bloodhound. I dislike the fact Patricia has the upper hand over me. I must find out her next move and beat her to the punch to stop her madness. Patricia has an overwhelming hatred against me. Where does it stem from, and why is she determined to make me suffer? I've thought it over and over again. I don't have any answers. I remember something my divinity school teacher shared with us about the truth. He said that finding the truth in any situation requires examining things that may seem unrelated. No stone should be left unturned. Sometimes, the truth is right before us and will set us free. If the truth is right before me, I must look closer to find it. My sister left her vehicle here in case of an emergency. I believe finding the truth is an emergency.

"Good afternoon, pastor."

"Good afternoon. You're bright and early today. Are you ready to go out and pray over the sick?"

"Somewhat, but I have a lot on my mind."

"Would you like to share it with me?"

"I don't know if I can. If I share it with you, I will break my trust."

"Son, if something's bothering you, talking about it might help."

"I'm just confused. I'm not sure what to do."

"What are you confused about?"

"It's my fiancée," the elder pastor grins.

"Oh, you're confused about marriage. Having second thoughts?"

"No, I love her completely. It's about her brother."

"She has a brother?"

"Yes, I found out yesterday."

"What's his name?"

"Paul Mitchell," the minister's eyes widen.

"Pastor Paul Mitchell, the one in the asylum?"

"Yes, but he's not in the asylum anymore. He's escaped. My fiancée brought him to my apartment yesterday, and he's there right now as we speak," the elder pastor shakes his head.

"You're harboring a fugitive inside your apartment? Son, if the police find out, you will go to jail."

"I know, but I promised Sharon not to tell," the elder pastor rubs his hands together.

"You have a difficult situation, but you must consider your future. If the police find Paul there, your career will be over like his."

"What happened to him?" The older pastor sighs.

"Sit down, son; this might take a minute. What made you decide to be a pastor?"

"The lord spoke to me in a dream. And even before that happened to me, God put me in circumstances where I had to administer and advise people in trouble. I felt linked to the human condition."

"Were you ever influenced by anyone else other than God?"

"No," the elder pastor draws the blinds to his office, letting in the sun. He peers out into the warm sunlight.

"You know, son, I was called also. Many of us are. Some then become ministers because of influence. Paul had big shoes to fill. His father was an awesome, charismatic preacher. When this man opened his mouth to preach, his delivery and how he tied scripture to current events was masterful. It was like watching a genius at his craft. God, without a doubt, chose him."

"He was that good?"

"He was better than good, if there is such a thing. Paul Mitchell Senior was the talk of the town. His followers would come to his house for prayer and worship. He never turned anyone down. If he were available, he would help them. He even gave out food to people experiencing homelessness and advocated for social injustice. But then someone took his life. It is part of why his son decided to become a preacher. He wanted to honor his father. I don't believe he was called to preach. It was a lot of pressure on him to follow in his father's footsteps. For a while, he was holding it together pretty nicely. He even had some followers comparing him to his dad. I once heard him preach, and his sermon moved me."

"What happened then?"

"Patricia Martin happened. She interrupted his ministry. He spent less time in the pulpit and more time entertaining her."

"He told me that part, but how did he end up in a mental asylum?"

"The man lost his mind. The police had tons of evidence pointing in his direction. She said he raped and beat her nearly half to death. Some pictures showed how badly she looked. When they arrested him, he was standing on the Brooklyn Bridge, threatening to jump. I'll never forget the look on his face and the screaming."

"Screaming?"

"He was shouting out words that sounded like babble. When the police approached him, he climbed further up the bridge. At that point, the officers didn't know what to do. One officer stated it was as if he was following someone to the top of the bridge. After nearly an hour, he climbed the bridge and spoke in tongues. It took five officers to hold him down and take him into custody. His speaking was unintelligible for at least a week after his arrest. No one could understand him. The display he showed on the bridge made us all believe he raped and beat Patricia. He did a job on that gal."

"So you believe her?" The elder pastor slides his black bible over and sits at his mahogany desk.

"I don't want to believe her, but the pictures convinced me. That man has an evil side to him."

"What about if she's lying, sir?"

"Son, he wrote letters to her. He became obsessed when he couldn't have her. I guess he figured if he couldn't have her, then no one else could."

"I didn't know. Paul seems like an okay person."

"There are many wolves in sheep's clothing."

"What do you suggest I do?"

"I think you should turn him in."

"My fiancée will never forgive me."

"If he hurts another woman, you will never forgive yourself either."

"I guess you're right."

"Some decisions in life require a sacrifice, son," Brandon removes his cell phone from his pocket.

"9-1-1, what's your emergency?"

"I want to report an escape."

The brown Victorian home sits on a dead-end street. I park my sister's truck inside the narrow cul-de-sac. The house has the same familiarity as it did when I was a child. It's hard to believe I haven't seen this place in five months. My mother's silver crown Victoria sits in the driveway. I climb the five squeaky porch stairs to reach the screen door. When I reach out to ring the doorbell, the screen door opens. My mother greets me with a nasty scowl of an expression.

"What do you want?" She yells through the screen.

"Mama, I need to talk to you."

"I don't have a son anymore. My son died five months ago."

"Mama, I know I made a mistake. I'm not perfect."

Chapter 32

China

China's statement stunned the two detectives. The detectives didn't expect to hear her say the bodyguard didn't rape her. What was more baffling for the detectives is she admitted being raped by her boyfriend instead. The short detective realizes rape victims thinking can sometimes become disoriented and delusional after a traumatic event has happened to them. He has to make sure she is telling the truth. Sending a man to jail for rape is a grievous charge.

"China, the doctor implied your bodyguard raped you. If your boyfriend raped you, why would he stick around and bring you to the hospital for treatment?" China shuts her eyes and thinks of something convincing to say.

"He felt guilty for what he did to me. He even threatened me not to tell anyone," the shorter detective listens intensely.

"What were you two talking about before he left the room?"

"He wanted to remind me what would happen if I told the truth."

"And what might that be?" The taller detective asks.

"He said if I told anyone, my life would be in grave danger."

"Well, there you have it. I think China is telling the truth," the shorter detective is unsure. He continues his questioning.

"China, your boyfriend doesn't have any marks on his face. Did you put up a fight when he raped you?" The taller detective glances at the shorter detective and sighs.

"Can't you see how big he is? I tried to fight, but he was too strong for me. The man can bench press over three hundred pounds. I only weigh 130."

"Why did you tell the doctor your bodyguard raped you then?" A tear runs down her cheek.

"He forced me to say that. I had no choice."

"China, you don't have to answer any more questions. We have enough information to arrest him with," the taller detective suggests. She doesn't like how the shorter one stares at her, his eyes never leaving hers. China starts crying more and more to persuade them.

"I can't walk, for God's sake, and he took advantage of me! He said it's been months since we had sex together. He just couldn't wait any longer, so he forced himself inside of me. It hurts me to keep talking about it. Do I have to answer any more questions?" She cries.

"You certainly do not. We've heard enough. I know you must be terrified. You don't have to worry anymore. We will place Mark under arrest," the shorter detective isn't buying it, but he goes along with the lead detective. The detectives leave the room and approach Mark.

"Mr. Chambers?"

"Yes, is she ok?" He stands up to greet the detectives.

"You under arrest!"

"What are you talking about?"

"What am I talking about?"

"You don't remember? How can you rape a woman and forget that easily?" The taller of the two suggests.

"I didn't rape her. Her bodyguard did."

"Tell it to the judge. You're under arrest for the rape of China Reynolds. You have the right to remain silent. Anything you say can be used against you in a court of law. You have a right to an attorney. If you can't afford one, the state will provide one for you," Mark balls his fists together. "I suggest you make this as easy as possible, Mr. Chambers," Mark unclenches his fists, turning around with his hands behind his back to be handcuffed.

"Can I say something to her?" Mark pleads.

"What for?" The taller detective asks.

"I would like to tell her I'm sorry."

"So, you admit to raping her then?"

"I didn't rape her. I want to tell her I'm sorry for abandoning her when she needed me the most."

"Nice try, buddy, but you're going straight to jail."

"Not so fast," the shorter detective interrupts.

"Harry, he raped her. Why should we let him see her? She's under enough stress already."

"Kevin, he only wants to apologize. How much can that hurt? He will probably never see her again."

"Harry, I'm only giving in because of you. Mr. Chambers, you have two minutes."

"I appreciate that." When the two detectives escort Mark back inside the room, China cannot look him in the face. Her guilt is tearing away at her. She is sending an innocent man to jail.

"China, I'm sorry for not being there for you when you needed me the most. You neglected me, China. I felt left out of your life. I became attached to you. It was more than just the hype. I fell in love with China, the person, not the megastar. I could've done a whole lot more to strengthen our relationship. I should've been there for you when you lost your ability to walk. I'm sorry. I understand you are upset, but to charge me with rape is ridiculous. I've always respected you. I've been with you for five years. How in the hell can you do this to me?"

"Calm down, Mr. Chambers. You have one minute left," China turns her head to look out the window.

"I know what this is all about. You want Jason, don't you? You always have. You're protecting him by having me arrested? He will hurt you again, China. Mark my words. This rape thing won't stick. I will get out. And when I do, I will expose him," China continues to ignore Mark.

"Ok, Mr. Chambers, time is up. Let's go." As they leave the room, Detective Harry glances over at China. Her face has widespread uneasiness written all over it. She is lying, and he knows it. She's in love with the bodyguard. Maybe it happened during the rape or before the rape. One thing was for sure: she couldn't hide it. He will not let an innocent man go to jail. Mark Chambers isn't a rapist. The tabloids called him everything else but never a rapist.

China feels guilty about her decision. She will tell the police the truth later. For now, she needs to spend more time with Jason. Her true sweetheart has been right in front of her. How could she have been so blind not to notice him? Jason traveled with her everywhere, her second pair of eyes. She remembers when he first came on board as her bodyguard. China interviewed three other men, along with Jason. She asked a series of questions about security. Jason's response to the inquiries made her feel protected compared to the others. In one particular question, he said he would give his life if it meant saving hers. The other three candidates weren't willing to sacrifice their life for her. Jason straightforwardly acquired the job over the other three prospects. Since then, he's never been late and hasn't missed a day of duty. His commitment to safeguarding her is extraordinary. He knows her exact whereabouts at all times. Jason makes mental notes of important dates and appointments. He makes sure the perimeters of her travel destinations have the appropriate security. China wonders if Jason can perform the same way as her man. Will he stay by her side when she needs him the most? Will Jason remember their anniversary or her birthday? Will he remain close to her and keep her from feeling lonely? Only time will tell.

DAVID

33

"Can you believe it, David? She just told the entire state of Connecticut about your attempted suicide. What happened to your privacy rights? She has no right to do this. What kind of journalist is she to do this to you? You demand better. I'm going out there right now to give her a piece of my mind."

"Cathy, don't waste your time. It's not important to me. It's only words."

"It's more than just words. Danita's words shape the opinion of those who are listening. The public will form assumptions about you as a person. You heard it as clearly as I did. She just asked the television viewers how you can take your life when you have more than enough to be thankful for. The media will destroy your character; the worst part is everyone knows you're here. It's a mad house out there."

"I don't care anymore, Cathy. My life has taken a turn for the worse. I know you think I'm crazy in all for wanting to kill myself."

"I don't think you're crazy, David. You just had some bad breaks."

"I've had bad breaks my entire life. Sometimes, I wonder why life exists if we have to suffer so much. It's pointless. From birth, we can't walk, talk, or care for ourselves without someone helping us; when our independence arrives, it is short-lived because the years pass so quickly. Once again, we're back to where we started and relying on others to care for us because we're too frail to do so. In between the aging process, we suffer from illnesses, loss of loved ones, setbacks, catastrophic events, and loneliness. If we weren't born, none of this would happen to us," Cathy turns off the television. She gently touches David's bandages.

"David, isn't it better to have lived than not to have lived at all?"

"What has living done for me? Look at me, Cathy. Just look at me. What has living done for me?"

"I can't imagine how you feel. But I do know that others are suffering more than you. As a doctor, David, I've seen my share of pain. I've seen babies born without limbs. Children as young as six years old with brain tumors. I've seen the bodies of babies as young as two years old after molestation. Just last week, a single mother of three arrived at the hospital with a flesh-eating disease. David, it was awful. She was withering away, and there wasn't anything we could do to save her. She kept mumbling about her children. She didn't want to leave her children."

"After witnessing so much pain regularly, how can you continue to perform your job?"

"I have a purpose in life. We all have a purpose. I strongly believe we belong in places for a reason. It's not by chance or coincidence. The fact you're here right now means something."

"What the hell does it mean? Please enlighten me."

"I don't know, but don't give up. Not just yet. I will help you through this. I promise."

"I have a slew of problems."

"You have given into negative thinking. Stay positive, David. Your life isn't over yet. You're here for something."

"And what might that something be?"

"I wish I knew David. I believe in time, you will find out. Just promise me one thing."

"I don't like to make promises I can't keep. What's the promise you want me to make?"

"I want you to promise me you will never attempt suicide again."

"I don't know if I can promise you that. It depends."

"It depends on what?"

"Whatever else comes my way in the meantime?"

"What's that supposed to mean?"

"You should be able to answer it better than I can. You're the one attending church and worshipping a God. What does your God have for me next?"

"David, you need to be careful with your choice of words. God can hear you."

"I'm not afraid, Cathy. He's not real, anyway. He would not have let these things happen to me if he were real."

"I refuse to argue with you. I'm just here to give you the support you need," a knock on the door interrupts Cathy's conversation.

"Come in," David says. Detective Harry and Detective Kevin enter and introduce themselves.

"David, we are here to ask you some questions about your suicide attempt. Our main concern is the firearm used. Can you tell us more about the gun? How did you know of the gun's location, and what made you decide to use a gun to take your life? I know you're under a lot of stress, so take your time. My partner and I will not pressure you. You can start anytime you're ready," David has a repulsed look. Cathy touches his hand.

"It's ok, honey. The police said you can take your time. Whenever you're ready," David rubs his hands over his face and takes in a deep breath, then releases it with a noticeable groan heard across the room.

"I'm ready."

"Are you certain? Cathy asks. There's no rush."

"Yes," he starts to explain. I knew of the gun's location since I was a child. My uncle had a special hiding place for it. I stumbled upon the silver thirty-eight special one day while playing with my football in the kitchen. I never told him I knew where he hid the gun. He used to take me out to a deserted field and fire off some rounds. Not once did he ever let me hold it. He worried about my welfare. With all the shit going on in my life, I figure, why not use the gun to end it all."

"Were you surprised to find the nine millimeters in the hiding place instead of the thirty-eight special?"

"It was odd initially, but I wasn't concerned about it. I assumed my uncle wanted a more up-to-date weapon. I just needed the gun to fire. I didn't dwell on the difference."

"Is it safe to say you knew nothing about the gun?"

"I had never touched the gun until that moment."

"Do you believe Keisha had anything to do with the gun being there?"

"I doubt it."

"When we questioned her, she claimed she removed the gun years ago. Keisha told us she hates guns. She demanded Chuck to lock his gun away and keep it out of sight from anyone to get their hands on it."

"Was there anyone else in the house besides you and Keisha?"

"Her son Nate," Cathy raises an eyebrow.

"Detective, may I say something?"

"Sure, and who may I ask, are you?"

"My name is Cathy Shaw. I'm a close friend," Detective Harry nods.

"What can you add to this?"

"I don't know if it will help, but Nate did not look happy when I came into the room to see David. It might not sound like much, but I think he wanted to hurt David."

"C'mon Cathy, let it go. Nate and I lived together at one time. We ate at the same dinner table, played on the same athletic teams, and shared the same chores. My casa was his casa."

"If that's true, then it shouldn't bother him if we ask him a few questions since you are so close. Has there ever been a fallout between the two of you?"

"Once, but it was a long time ago."

"How long ago would you say?"

"We were both teenagers then. It upset him that I dated his girlfriend before he met her."

"What makes you believe he was upset?"

"The girl I dated before him told me afterward. He broke ties with her. She loved my stepbrother. She wanted things to work out, but Nate ended it. He stayed away from me after that."

"Have you ever spoken to him about this?"

"No. At that time, I was too busy with other things. I had girls chasing after me. I figured he would bounce back like I always did after a breakup. Do you think because of this, he would want to harm me?"

"You can never tell. I've seen stranger motives. It kind of makes sense, though. Keisha called Nate to watch you when she found you on the kitchen floor. She knew about the thirty-eight for some time. Keisha pretended not to notice you in search of the gun. She told us about your conversation with her in the car about not wanting to live. The slit underneath the floor was empty, to her knowledge. We have the thirty-eight in our possession, along with the nine millimeter. Her story adds up. At this point, we need to question Nate. And one more thing, David, someone used the nine millimeter in a local murder. The serial number is missing. If Nate purchased this gun from a street dealer, he's looking at some serious consequences facing him."

"He mentioned something about the gun purchased off the street."

"What will happen to David for trying to take his life with the same gun?" Cathy asks.

"We are certain David did not know about the gun before using it. He will be assigned to a psychiatrist and further evaluated."

Dissatisfied with seeing David alive, Nate walks through the mob of spectators standing in front of the hospital. Once again, his stepbrother gets attention even in a failed suicide attempt. Since they were children, David appealed to people and quickly angered Nate. How did the bullet not kill him? Nate wonders. Nate dwells on the beautiful woman inside the room with David and thinks of another way. An eye for an eye, a tooth for a tooth, a woman for a woman will make it even.

PAUL

34

"Mom, I need you to trust me."

"Trust you? You're a fugitive, for Christ's sake. Your father is probably turning over in his grave as we speak. God bless his soul."

"Mom, how do you know that I'm a fugitive? Did Sharon tell you this?"

"No, her boyfriend did."

"He said he was sorry for calling the police and had no choice."

"He did have a choice. I knew it was risky. I told Sharon not to involve him. She said I could trust him. I explained my situation to him. I thought he believed me."

"He's a good man. You can't blame him for calling the police. In his mind, you're a dangerous man. He did the right thing. My house is probably the second place they'll look for you. I don't think you should have come here. Why did you come here anyway?"

"I came to explain the real story to you. It would be nice if you would just listen to me for once."

"Listen to you?" Did you listen to me when I told you to leave that woman alone? You embarrassed our family, Paul Jr. How could you do this to us? I can't even show my face in the church without hearing about your failures. The congregation has written you off. They have nothing but contempt for you."

"Mom, do you think I care what people say about me? The same people digging my grave are probably doing the worst things. I know the truth, and God knows the truth."

"How dare you mention God? You turned your back on God; look where it has brought you. Our family is one of faith. We pray and wait for God to rescue us when obstacles arise. No weapon or calamity formed against us shall prosper when God is with us. Your life is in chaos because you abandoned the lord. I knew she wasn't right when you brought that woman over here. I told you to distance yourself from her, but you wouldn't listen. You lost everything chasing after her tail."

"Mom, I didn't rape her. Just listen to me. Yes, I had sex with her. I wanted her more than anything. I fell for her quickly and assumed she felt like I did for her. When I learned she falsely accused me of rape, I was devastated. There were no warning signs. Our relationship was perfect. Then, out of nowhere, she turns on me."

"She was never right from the start. I could sense it. You let her stir you away from preaching. Several members told me how your words inspired them to do much more with their lives and to be faithful Christians. When the congregation learned of your arrest, many of the members felt betrayed and left the church for good," my mother's disgusted manifestation exposes her age. Looking at her, I think the five months I spent in Bedford have aged her. She appears to have more wrinkles and gray hair than I can remember. "Tell me something, Paul Jr., how did you come to lose your mind?"

"Mom, I didn't lose my mind."

"If you didn't lose your mind, why were you placed in a mental institution?"

"It's because I attempted suicide."

"Doesn't that suggest you lost your mind?"

"Not entirely," she looks befuddled.

"Were you on drugs?"

"Mom, I'm not an addict."

"Were you on any kind of prescription drugs at the time?"

"No."

"Let me get this straight. You don't do drugs, and you weren't on any prescription meds, but you attempted suicide? Son, nothing was influencing you but you."

"I guess I had a slight meltdown, but I'm not crazy. I'm your son. You know what kind of person I am."

"I used to know you. The son I knew would've never attempted suicide, especially a pastor of the church."

"Mom, aren't you forgetting something?"

"Forgetting what?"

"If you're going to tell the story, tell it all. Don't leave out bits and pieces. As I recall, you nearly lost your mind when my father died. You couldn't eat for weeks. You lost so many pounds. You were in a deep state of depression. Sharon and I had to work hard to nurse you back to reality," she stares at me disparagingly.

"How dare you bring up your father's death to make a point? Your father was a vessel for God. The Lord sent him an angel to help him."

"An angel?"

"Paul Jr., let me finish telling you."

"Mom, wait, what did this angel look like?"

"What does it matter to you what he looked like? Your faith is weak. You have lost your way. Just let me finish telling you so you can do whatever you do," she shakes her head in disgust.

"I saw an angel too," she gathers herself together. Her eyes widen.

"When did this happen, Paul Jr.?"

"The night I tried to kill myself. He was there. He talked me out of it. He said I had so much more to do, and it wasn't my time to go yet."

"Glory be to God. The time has finally come! I've waited years for this moment. My mother instantly drops to her knees, thanking the lord.

"Mom, why are you on your knees thanking the lord?"

"I was reluctant to give you the information. I had to wait until the time was right."

"I don't understand. What are you talking about?"

"The angel, your father said this would be the sign."

"A sign for what?"

"Healing. You can heal. You've always had it along with your ancestors," my mother's words astound me. I think her age is finally catching up to her. She looks somewhat lost, and her hair is messy. I help her up from the floor. "Paul Jr., you don't have much time. I will tell you what I know. Listen to me very carefully. Your great-grandfather, grandfather, and father had healing capabilities. You have it, too. You've always had it. I don't remember the exact age you were then, but I think seven or eight. I remember you coming home telling your dad that one of your classmates fell off the monkey bars during recess. You went on to explain to us your classmate had broken his right leg. He came to school the next day with his leg in a cast. Paul Jr., you were one of the most excellent boys in the class. The teachers raved about how smart and polite you were. They called you their little helper. Whenever someone struggled to do anything in class, you would volunteer to help them. When your friend fell from the monkey bars, it upset you. He was sort of your play partner when it was time for recess. You came home after his injury and told your father and me you didn't have anyone to play with. You complained about the cast not being removed for at least five weeks. We suggested you play with other kids, but you only wanted to play with Pete. I think one of your father's sermons in church might have inspired you to do what you did in school. The week before your classmate's accident, your father preached about gifts bestowed upon us by the lord. As it is written in the bible, each of us has a different skill to offer others. Some are led to teach, some are led to preach, some are led to assist those with needs, and some are shown to heal.

The next day after school, you came home a little disappointed. I asked what was bothering you. You said you put your hands on your classmate's cast and prayed for God to heal him, but nothing happened. Me, being a mother, I embraced you. I didn't want you to be upset or lose faith in God. I said give it some time. God works in his time, not our time. I figured you would probably forget about it in a few days, as most children do with most things. Danny was jumping around in his cast the next day in school. The teachers almost had a heart attack.

They called his parents because he wouldn't stay off his injured leg. He said he felt fine, and his leg had no more pain. The doctors were against cutting open the cast, but the boy was adamant about his pain vanishing. Reluctantly, they took off the cast. An x-ray revealed his leg was perfectly normal. The doctors couldn't explain it. Neither could anyone else. Your father and I understood the truth," I look into my mother's eyes and see a sparkle of light, a sense of hope for humankind. The very same sparkle that had been projected from her eyes when my father had preached his sermons.

"Paul Jr., do you know what this means?" The enthusiasm spreads through her face.

"I'm not sure I do."

"It means you can carry on your father's legacy and let God use you to save others," I stand before my mother in question. I've been in a psychiatric ward for the last five months, living among mentally ill patients. Twenty-four hours prior, I witnessed Alexandria's dead body. I've injured Sage in a torture chamber created by a psychopathic doctor. The police are looking for me. My ex-girlfriend continues to haunt me, and my mother is telling me I have the power to heal. Her information is problematic for me to swallow.

"Your father told me to confide in you when right. He said that if an angel approaches you, that would be the sign. How many times did you see this angel?"

"I saw him only once."

"What did he look like?"

"He looked like a regular man, except for his eyes and the widespread joy on his face. I saw an image of myself through his crystal clear eyes and a vision of my father."

"Your father was also visited by this same angel many times during his healing journey. I wanted to share this information with you for a long time, but I had to be certain. From what you've just shared, I'm convinced you have the same ability as your father."

"I'm just a man, mom, a troubled man with many problems. Even if I could heal, how can I focus on saving others when my life is in dire straits?"

"Son, you haven't been away from the pulpit all that long. It's only been five months. Where is your faith? The devil tests us when things in our lives are chaotic. He wants us to give up and to give in to him, but I know a God who says the devil is a lie. Put Satan behind you and carry out your works. Serve man, give to the needy, feed the hungry, clothe the naked, and save souls from despair. If you do this for the lord, the things in your life will fall into place," my mother sounds like my father. I guess what they say about a strong man is true. He has a strong woman behind him.

"You're not the only one with problems. Your father, God blesses his soul, had difficulties as high as the sky. He never let that stop him."

"I have to clear my name of all wrongdoing."

"Son, when the angel first appeared to your father, we struggled to survive? Our bills were months past due. We were behind in our mortgage. The bank had repossessed one of our cars, and your father and I mostly argued over finances. The small church in which your father and I started didn't grow as quickly as we expected it to in the beginning. The members came sparingly to church. It was a low point in our life. Paul Senior was ready to give up when the angel appeared before him. He told your father to give his burdens to God, and everything would be alright. Your father did what the angel instructed him to do. He worked harder than I had ever seen him work on saving people. In that short time, God blessed us with more than we could ever imagine, but it did come with a price. He lost his life in the process," her serious face returns.

"I can't even show my face. Did you forget I'm a wanted man? I escaped from a mental institution. How can I come into contact with anyone? They will know who I am."

"I don't know, Paul Jr. I didn't say it would be easy. You have to figure it out."

"How am I supposed to do that?" She leaves the room, returning with a black journal.

"What's this?"

"It's your father's notes and his gateway into healing. Everything you need to know is in there."

"Have you read it?"

"Your father strictly forewarned me not to read it. It's for your eyes only."

Bedford Mental Institution

"I miss you so much. I want to see you today. I wish I didn't have to attend this stupid emergency meeting at work."

"What happened at work?"

"A patient escaped from the asylum. And get this; he murdered a patient before escaping."

"Who?"

"The crazy pastor, the one I told you about. His name is Paul Mitchell. People will believe in anything these days. How is it possible he led a congregation? These so-called ministers are nothing but charlatans."

"Did they find him yet?"

"No, the police are covering the state looking for him. He may strike again if someone doesn't pick him up soon."

"Maybe someone will put an end to him before he gets another chance."

"Patricia, I sure do hope so. He deserves the most horrible outcome."

"Who did he kill Francine?"

"Alexandria. It's so sad. Everyone at the facility liked her. How could he kill her? I just don't understand any of it. It doesn't make sense to me. I know they were together a lot."

"They could've had a lover's quarrel."

"I've never seen them argue, though. The two seemed very happy around each other."

"Francine, please be careful. I think you should start looking for another place of employment. It's unsafe to continue working there, especially with psychopaths running around."

"I'll be careful. Will I see you later on?"

"I'm swamped today."

"For the past week, you've been busy. When are you going to make time for us? I love you. You're all I think about lately. It's not fair to me that I can't see you. I want to be with you right now."

"Francine, I know it's been a while since we last held each other. Stop fretting so much. You know how I am. I might show up and surprise you at your meeting."

"You will? She asks, overly excited.

"You never know."

"Patricia, you know how I like surprises. Please don't make me wait any longer. I'm miserable without you. What have you done to me? No matter how hard I try, I can't get you out of my mind."

"Francine, you'll be fine. I'll see you sooner than you think."

"I hope so. I can't take it anymore. I love you."

"I love you too."

Paul Mitchell is a fugitive running for his life. The thought of his desperate situation makes her heart dance. He can hide in only a few places, and Patricia knows all of them. His life will soon be over. Her justice will come shortly. Lethal injection has a nice ring to it. Her job is complete. It's time for her to sit back and enjoy the show with the rest of the world watching.

CHINA

35

Mark has never seen the inside of a jail cell before. He has heard stories of how depressing it is and the charted dangers. The small holding cell reeks of urine. There are three others in the cell beside him: a young black kid who looks no more than sixteen with a swollen face, a hung-over elderly white man, and a tall black woman who keeps wiping her eyes. At this point, Mark can care less about who they are or their story for being placed behind bars. His focus remains on Jason. The thought of him touching China makes him furious. He realizes China isn't in her right state of mind to charge him with raping her. Jason has his claws in her. Mark realizes in due time, Jason will tear her apart if given the chance. He cannot sit idle in a jail cell and allow her to die. He must do something. Mark walks to the front of the cell. He bangs his fists against the bars to draw attention. A white female officer approaches.

"Hey, what's your problem?" She unpleasantly asks.

"I need to see the detective."

"May I ask what for?"

"I rather not say. It's a private matter. I just need to talk to the detective, and it's important," she scans him over.

"Normally, I don't do favors for criminals, but I've seen you countless times in the news. I think you and China make a great couple. My friends and I made wagers on how long you would last. Most of us couldn't believe a superstar as big as her would even give you the time or the day. We didn't think you would've made it this long. You surprised all of us. I credit you for hanging in there with so much negative press directed toward you. I know it's none of my business, but I just have to know. What is it like dating a person widely known as her?"

"It's no different than dating anyone else. China is human. People make the rich and famous more than what they appear to be. She puts her clothes on the same way as you and I. The only difference is she has a bigger wardrobe," the female officer laughs lightheartedly.

"You know something; you're pretty down to earth. I like that. I will get the detective for you."

"Thank you," in a brief moment, Detective Harry approaches the holding cell. His dark brown hair ruffled a bit. His white shirt has coffee stains near the collar, and his rust-colored Khakis have wrinkles. His bloodshot eyes look as if he hasn't slept in days.

"What can I do for you, Mark?"

"I'm innocent. You know I am."

"I'm innocent too. And don't forget me. And me too," the three cellmates detest.

"Hey, tell it to the judge, you three," Detective Harry says, returning his attention to Mark.

"If you don't do something fast, he'll probably end up killing her. She's not in her right state of mind."

"I hate to be the bearer of bad news, but from the looks of things, I'd say she's in love with him."

"I thought the same thing initially, but she denied it."

"Maybe it happened after he raped her," Mark frowns.

"How the hell do you fall in love with someone after they physically assault you?"

"Her situation is different from most because of their time together over the years. Jason knows everything about her, and she's comfortable around him. Maybe in some weird way, she wanted to experience more of him other than Jason being her bodyguard."

"You're not making this any easier for me, detective."

"I know, but when I observed her body language in the hospital, I couldn't help but notice how love-struck she looked. I study people for a living. It's my job. She's protecting him because she's very fond of him. She'll probably drop the charges against you once she reunites with him," Mark backs away from the bars as if it's electrically charged.

"In a way, I believed it. I just didn't want it to be true. If you knew this, why didn't you arrest him instead of me?"

"My partner is the senior detective on the case. I work under him. Normally, he's never wrong when judging a person, but I think this time he is. I did a little digging into Jason's past. It was a challenge, but I found some dirt on this guy. It's not his first time attacking a woman. He's done it three other times, and he's gotten away each time. He's good at what he does. Jason is an ex-navy seal. He's done a few tours in Iraq. Jason was once a leading candidate for a secret service position."

"What happened to the position?

"After a navy secretary filed a sexual harassment complaint, he lost his chance to protect and serve the president. The report states he made her very uncomfortable. He caressed her quite often inside the barracks. She also claimed he almost raped her on one occasion, but she managed to get away."

"I knew there was something wrong with this guy. I just couldn't put my finger on it."

"It gets better. The report also says Jason broke into her apartment and confiscated her panties, stockings, and some photos of herself at the beach in a bikini."

"This guy is a real pervert. Let me guess, the charges dropped?"

"Jason had an excellent lawyer. He denied everything. His lawyer sued the Navy for falsely accusing him of sexual harassment and his disqualification from the secret service."

"Did they win?" The detective gives Mark a "what do you think" expression.

"How, with all the evidence pinned against him?"

"I take it you've never seen LA law, have you?"

"I'm not a big fan of lawyers. I think they're slippery as snakes."

"It's called reasonable doubt. If a jury can smell it, the case can swing the other way immediately, tipping the scale of justice."

"How much reasonable doubt are we talking about?"

"Let's say, two million dollars' worth."

"Why is he working for China? It's not like he needs the money."

"Remember Mark, this guy is military. He needs a challenge—something to keep his mind occupied. I've spoken with ex-militia enough to know they hate downtime. Sitting idle after years of combat with nothing to do drove some soldiers crazy."

"It seems to me he's already there."

"You're probably right. It's my job to prevent Jason from attacking her again."

"Has he ever been accused of killing anyone?" Detective Harry doesn't want to burden Mark. He steps closer to the cell, choosing his words precisely.

"There was this one time written in the report where his girlfriend entered the emergency room for life-threatening injuries. A vehicle rammed her off a deserted road into a tree, mangling her car. She scarcely survived the crash. His girlfriend insisted he was inside the car that drove her off the road. He became enraged after learning of his girlfriend's exotic dancing at a local strip joint. If Jason was the perpetrator, the police never found his vehicle, and he once again denied it."

"How can he continue to attack women and keep getting away with it?"

"In previous cases, the victims were too afraid to press charges against him. He walked away scot-free. In the case of China, I don't think she's afraid of him. I think he sparked something in her. To you and me, it might sound outlandish for a woman to desire a man right after he rapes her. But if you think about it briefly, he knew the precise buttons to push. He's been around her a relatively long time. He understands her likes and dislikes. What we call rape, he may consider it to be the common behavior."

"He's sick. You know that just plain sick in the head."

"China is curious. I think she wants to know how far the rabbit hole goes. Women seem to think they can change a man no matter how screwed up they are."

"So what will you do, detective?"

"There's little I can do without her pressing any charges. I need a statement from her, and I don't believe she's ready to give us one."

"What about me?"

"I suggest you stay put and wait until you face the judge. Hopefully, you can make bail by then. It will be difficult for you. Rape is a grim charge. Most judges on the circuit are strictly against it. If it's a female judge, God help you."

China's invite startles Jason. He repeatedly plays the voice message until he is satisfied with its authenticity. He immediately becomes aroused after hearing her voice once more. He needs to see her again. When he abandoned China on the bedroom floor, leaving her in disarray, he estimated that the night he'd spent with her would probably be his last. Jason expected China to have pure hatred for him after he physically attacked her. He prepared himself for any outcome, knowing the police would be hunting for him. To his amazement, for China to contact him must have meant she also enjoyed it. In the beginning, she screamed for him to stop. It brought him enormous pleasure watching her squirm to free herself. After striking her face, something altered his hostility. He stopped abruptly in the middle of his onslaught, becoming apologetic and caring. She momentarily passed out. He then touched her body intimately, reviving her and letting euphoria take over. China responded to his caressing. She squeezed him tighter, pulling his body closer to hers. They kissed and feverishly made love to each other. This softer side agitates Jason. It goes against everything he learned growing up.

Letting his guard down during a time in his life had cost him so much pain and misery, his heart broken more times than he cared to remember. His friends called him Mr. Softy in those earlier years. He was easy, and the girls he met used him. They toyed with Jason, using mind games to keep him unaware of their devious objectives. He was a victim of them spending his money, sleeping with other guys behind his back, and bossing him around whenever they felt the need to. Jason is a true romantic. He believes in love at first sight. To Jason, women are beautiful creatures and deserve the best. When he stumbled upon his fiancée with another man by her side in the mall, he believed her story of how she was showing her distant cousin around the city. He never questioned her true intentions. Eventually, she parted ways with Jason, breaking his heart and never returning the ring. Two years after that situation ended, he opened his soul to another.

She belittled Jason in public and kept him away from his friends. Her hen pecking stressed him, and her loud mouth never stopped complaining. Jason did everything he could to please her, which never satisfied her. In the end, she canceled Jason for a female instead. After that episode, he promised to stay single to avoid getting hurt. On his 24th birthday, a few of his close friends celebrated with him at a pool hall. The night was going swell as Jason was having a blast. Toasted was his friend's, but he refused to drink, being the designated driver. Jason bopped his head to the music while shooting pool. Amid all the excitement, he noticed a group of women playing their own game of pooling a table from where he and his friends were playing. The three ladies were beautiful, but Jason was determined to keep his promise.

His three pool buddies make advances one by one in hopes of finding out their names and exchanging numbers. The women aren't interested and kindly decline their offers. One of the women in the group has her eyes on Jason. She stares in his direction most of the night but has no such luck attracting him. Unaware of her agenda, Jason continues to enjoy himself. His friends convince him to have one drink toasting his 24th birthday. After making the toast, she uses the opportunity to get Jason's attention. She bumps into him on purpose, making her way to the restroom, which causes his glass to fall out of his hand. He quickly drops down and catches the drink before it hits the floor. She apologizes to Jason and introduces herself. He must be dreaming, Jason thinks, because the woman standing over him is unquestionably unique. She looks like a movie star, a cross between Kerry Washington and Zoe Saldana. The woman seizes Jason's drink out of his hand and places it on the pool table. She then grabs him by his hand, leading him to the front of the bar where the speakers are. He dances with her for what seems like an eternity while keeping his eyes transfixed on her lovely figure. When the music stops for the night, he is disappointed it has to come to an end. They exchange numbers before leaving the pool hall.

Their connection matured into something meaningful over the past several months. Jason ignores his promise of staying away from women to avoid getting hurt. In no time at all, they were married. It is perfect. They fit like a hand and glove until the marriage shockingly ends when he discovers his wife and brother sleeping together. This atrocity transforms him into a different kind of man, a man living with built-in pain after being led astray by women. From then on, he no longer plays the fool or Mr. Nice Guy. His pleasant demeanor becomes a thing of the past—his new identity boards on lust and violence. The love and kindness inside of him have eroded. Using physical force, he takes from women what he desires. He makes women pay for their lies and dishonesty. To Jason, they are nothing but liars, cheaters, and money-hungry whores. China's character constitutes something different. Unlike the other women he came across and maltreated, she managed to tame the beast within him. Will she change like the others had, or will she be there for him? He is unsure of the risk but is willing to take the chance.

DAVID

36

Many people came out, bidding their last farewells to Uncle Chuck. The players from David's youth team sit in the first two pews of the church, paying their respects. His entire team is present, except for Nate. It's difficult for David to believe Nate would deliberately try to hurt him. They are like brothers and walk the same stomping grounds as children. For the detectives and Cathy to insinuate Nate as being this gruesome character makes Chuck's funeral even more depressing. David would give anything just to see his uncle's face one last time. Chuck was the only person there for him throughout his youth. When David made the mistakes life often brings, Chuck gave him his undivided support. He never judged David for his shortcomings, as his mother's side of the family had done so usually. But instead, he embraced David. Chuck wasn't a pushover, either. If David did something wrong, he scolded and punished him like any other average parent. He refused to hold grudges against David, forgiving and forgetting his mistakes accordingly. The young, charismatic bishop giving the eulogy looks out over the congregation. He is impressed by the attendance of so many. He begins his short sermon.

"We sit here today in remembrance of Charles Parks. Many of us know him as Chuck. Chuck was the type of man who positively touched everyone when he met you. He volunteered his time working with youth on the football field. He inspired many of his players to become successful after football ended. I can personally attest to his humanity. Chuck mentored my son, and he has done numerous things for others. Everyone in this room has been affected in a good way by Chuck in some form or manner. My brief sermon today is titled Help. The letter "H" in help stands for having. The letter "E" in help stands for everlasting. The letter "L" in help stands for love. And the letter "P" in help stands for prospering. God has put everyone here for a purpose or reason. Chasing after success is not what Jesus had in mind. Christ is all-powerful, as we know. If he wanted to be rich, then rich would he be? If he wanted to destroy us all, we would exist no more. He set an example for us to follow. He dedicated his life to helping humankind. When things are past our capacity, we cry out for help. The world is crying out for help, also. Can't you hear it, congregation? The cries of the less fortunate, the cries of people experiencing homelessness, the cries of pregnant teens, the cries of abused children, and the cries of victims suffering from police brutality. The letter "H" in help stands for having the courage to assist your fellow man or woman in need. The letter "E" in help is an everlasting commitment to fulfilling your life purpose. The letter "L" in help stands for loving your fellow neighbor as you would love yourself. The letter "P" in help stands for prospering not for you but thriving to save someone less fortunate. What does it benefit a man to gain the world and lose his soul? Before you leave this sanctuary today, I want you to remember what Chuck stood for. He wasn't perfect, but he cared for others in ways that are sometimes not self-evident. God rest his soul."

After the sermon ended, Cathy escorted David to the casket one last time. She carefully guides his hands over Chuck's body. His deteriorating sense of touch inhibits him from feeling anything. A tear from David falls inside the casket.

"I will not give up, Uncle Chuck. I will fight this for you. You never quit on me, and I won't quit on you. I will find a way to change what has happened to me. Rest in peace, I will miss you."

"Keisha, I'm glad you were able to make the funeral. I can't imagine how you felt locked up. I take all the blame. I was weak, thinking of myself only."

"David, things happen. It always does. You'll bounce back, trust me. And another thing, it's not your fault. My son did this to me. Why would he do this? Chuck and I raised both of you boys together. I never treated you or him any differently. I accepted you the first time Chuck introduced you. I love you and Nate the same. I have no favoritism. I believe Nate envies you. He wants to be just like you, following in your footsteps. Nate doesn't have the same gifts as you. My son tried as hard as he could. We did so much for that boy, and this is how he repays us?" She begins to cry.

"Keisha, don't let it get to you. He'll come around eventually."

"It's just that so much has happened. I don't know what to do or where to go from here. I just lost my husband and probably my son," she wipes away the tears composing herself.

"David, is it ok if Cathy takes you back to the house? I need to be alone for a while. I have to clear my head. It's a lot for me to deal with right now."

"Sure, it's not a problem."

"I will give her directions on how to get there."

Cathy drives through the city of New Haven at a snail's pace. She is unfamiliar with the city streets. An impatient driver is tailgating her. She ignores the driver.

"David, your uncle has so many friends. The church was standing room only."

"I know. I lost count of how many people approached me; they knew everything about me. Uncle Chuck told his friends everything I ever did. Individually, they said they were very proud of my accomplishments. I wish he were still here. I need him now more than I ever did then."

"He's with you, David, in spirit. I'm sorry, David. Here I go again, right, bringing up the word."

"Don't apologize. I need to hear the word more often," On cue, Cathy pulls her car into a local fast food establishment as the driver behind her speeds away, giving her the finger. She turns off the engine.

"I know that smell from anywhere, don't tell me. Uncle Chuck and I came here all the time. Their soul food is the best in Connecticut. Oh, now I remember. It's Sandra's, am I right?"

"I guess the nose doesn't lie. You're correct."

"But why are we stopping here? I'm full from the food at the funeral. Don't tell me you're still hungry, Cathy?"

"No, I'm not hungry, David. I pulled in here to better understand what you said about the word."

"I figure, why keep running away from it? Nothing else seems to be working in my life. My condition isn't getting any better. I think I should try another approach," Cathy raises her hands, incapable of holding in her enthusiasm.

"If you don't mind me asking, David, what has changed your mind?"

"The sermon at the funeral changed my thinking. I'm no fan of preachers, but everything he said today seemed meant for me."

"What you're describing happens to us all. The preacher is God's messenger. He breaks down God's message into a language we can understand."

"I understood everything. For the first time in my life, I feel linked. The part that did it for me was the letter "P" in prospering. Instead of striving to achieve artificial success, we should increase our efforts to help someone. I don't want to leave this earth known for my achievements, but I want people to remember me as someone who dedicated their life to making someone's life better. I'm accepting God into my life. He is my salvation. With him, all things are possible. I have to stop feeling sorry for myself. There's someone out there needing my help. I may be blind and deteriorating slowly, but I can do something before I leave this earth. I have to try. Maybe this is what God wanted me to see. He had to get my full attention. My desire blinded me, and I will pray for him to heal me. In the meantime, I will devote myself to helping others. I feel much better now, and I'm glad I have you by my side," Cathy reaches over, giving David a hug and a big kiss.

"I'm proud of you. You're going to make me cry," in an instant, Cathy's door swings open. Nate grabs her by her hair. She screams for him to release her.

"Shut up, woman, or I will end your life right here," he sticks a gun into her side. David recognizes Nate's voice.

"Nate, what's this about? She hasn't done anything to you. Let her go!"

"She hasn't done anything to me, but you have. And she's part of you. I'm going to make her suffer the way you and your uncle made me suffer."

"Nate, what are you talking about? I was there for you when we were teens. I introduced you to my friends. I brought you along with me when I went to parties. I even helped you on the football field."

"Don't bring that football shit up, David. You and Chuck did nothing for me on the field except embarrass me. Your uncle just wanted my mother, so he put up with me. He praised you like a God. They all did. No one gave a damn about me, not even my mother. When you went away to college, they completely ignored me. Cathy tries to squirm free. If you move again, I'll shoot you. Now keep your fine ass still."

"Nate, can't we work this out somehow?"

"You want to work this out, blind man? The only thing I'm going to work out is this fine piece of ass. You'll never hear her voice again after I finish with her."

"Nate, I'm sorry about Manuela. I dated her before you met her. How can you hold something like that against me after many years have passed?"

"You should have told me. You could've told me when you came home from practice that evening."

"I didn't want to hurt you. Manuela was special to you because you brought her home to meet Uncle Chuck and Keisha."

"Why must you have everything? You always have it all. It's not right. Why do you always get the pretty ones, David? And I get stuck with women no one wants. Huh, can you answer that for me?"

"Nate, I'm very sorry."

"I know you're sorry. Your entire situation is sorry, isn't it? Just look at you. You can't see shit. You can't feel anything, and your football days are over. You're not even a man anymore. A man can take care of himself, David. You're more like a child, a little boy who needs people to do things for him," David slams his hands against the dashboard.

"How can you say that to me? If I were able to see you, I would beat the hell out of you right now."

"Is that so? Well, let me tell you something. The word "if" is a big word. If your uncle had treated me better, my life would be different. You wouldn't be in this situation if you didn't take Manuela away from me. The word if has failed me the same way it's failing your sorry ass right now. I think it's time for me to leave. She is so beautiful. Aren't you, honey?" He kisses her cheek. Cathy wipes his saliva from her face.

"Bruh, you sure do know how to pick them. I think this one is finer than the rest of the girls I've ever seen you with. It's too bad you can't see her. I can't keep my eyes off of her. Well, David, on that note, I will leave you to yourself. A crowd is starting to form. Have fun."

PAUL

37

The information I gathered from my mother disturbs me. As children, we witness the outward physical aging process of our parents but are incapable of seeing the inward deteriorating aging progression as it unfolds. My mother is slowly losing her mental capacity. She thinks I have healing power. Jesus of Nazareth displayed the same commands to his disciples and the multitudes of followers. I'm far from a prophet, nowhere near a saint, and barely surviving as a man. The Bible says God created man in his image, a replica of himself. He has given man the understanding to perform miracles as the disciples did after being taught by Jesus. The disciples gave up their worldly possessions and sacrificed their lives to follow Christ in faith.

They could perform miracles and cast out demons only when they were innocent as babes, with nothing binding them. Am I willing to give up my life to heal the sick and unfortunate? If I do this task, I will run for the rest of my life. I will never have a family to call my very own or witness my children growing into adulthood. Everyone will expect my help, bringing on pandemonium. I quickly kiss my mother on her cheek, leaving her house as I hear sirens in the distance. I head in the reverse direction towards the old abandoned church my parents built. Many memories plunge into my brain when I pull up near the building. Vivid memories of my father preaching his message among the congregation appear as if he's standing before me. I can feel his manifestation and hear his compelling voice.

When my parents put their efforts into constructing a church, they started with the most miniature building possible, unsure how many people would attend. They rented a storefront church, which held about one hundred fifty persons. As attendance grew and membership expanded, the search was on to find a more extensive structure. It wasn't long before they found a dilapidated building capable of being rebuilt. Formerly, the building was once a youth center in the city's heart. With high taxes and budget cuts forcing businesses to move abroad, not to mention a dwindling economy, the youth center could not survive. My parents worked their behinds off and used their savings to get the church in full swing. About a year later, it became the biggest church in New Haven—everyone who was someone attended. My parents' church became the talk of the town until my father died. I park in the rear parking lot of the church. An uncharacteristic feeling comes over me as I unlock the door and enter. Dense-laden cobwebs and dust particles surround the ceiling and walls. The room smells like damp wood and mold. There is a fraction of light inside the church coming from outside. Like Dorothy, I trail the lightened path, following the yellow brick road to see the wizard. In her case, the wizard was a fake, a con artist hiding among ordinary citizens to stay clear of the wicked witch. My journey is opposite of Dorothy's but somewhat comparable.

The wizard was my dad. Unlike the Wizard of Oz, his power did exist. He healed people and made them whole again. Dorothy was looking for a way out through the wizard, a chance to get home to her family. I am also looking for an opportunity. I'm searching for a second chance to redeem myself and correct the wrongs in my life. I go into my dad's office. His office brings back instantaneous remembrances. As a youth, I hung around my dad's office doing homework and playing games on his computer. I dust off his red leather chair, plopping down behind his desk. The sun outside is beginning to set. I drew the shade to let in more light.

I look around the room. It hasn't changed a bit. Everything is in its original position. My father's bookshelf made of timber is standing against the wall near the window above it. The collection of literature inside the bookshelf remains in alphabetical order. His many plaques and certificates hang from the tarnished white walls. I place the book my mother handed to me on the desk. I open the book and begin reading. After reading, there's not much light inside the office. The sun has completely set. I close the book, deciding it is time to leave. A bright white light appears in the corner of my father's office in front of his bookshelf. I cover my eyes from the blinding light. Out of the white light appears a man—the same man who convinced me not to jump from the bridge on that terrible evening.

"Don't be afraid," he says to me as I turn to leave the office.

"Who are you?" I ask, trying to gather my composure.

"I am Eden."

"Like the garden of Eden in the book of Genesis?"

"Yes."

"Are you an angel?"

"That I am."

"Why have you come to me?"

"Paul, do you remember our conversation on the bridge?"

"Yes, I remember it."

"Then you know you have much more work to do."

"Why, me and not someone else?"

"Paul, God has chosen you because of your ancestor's great deeds. It was their everlasting faith during the time of slavery that kept God with them. Your descendants aided the sick and cared for the wounded. Their inner strength to fight through impossible odds, though keeping their faith, earned God's compassion. He never left their side. He gave them the power of healing and the ability to cast out demons. As you may know from your history, millions of enslaved Africans died on ships setting out to America. And more of them were murdered and tortured once they reached the American shores. God kept his promise to your ancestors. He sanctified your bloodline, giving future offspring the same gifts. Your father and his father before him were progenies of this; the same blood that ran through their veins runs in yours. You have the same ability, the same gifts, and the very same knowledge. Even as a child, you had this gift."

"Is this possible?" Eden frowns.

"Paul, when you believe in God with all your heart, mind, and soul, there's no limitation on what you can do. Have you read the book?"

"I have."

"What have you learned from it?"

"I've learned what my father did is something I won't be able to do. I don't have his strength. I'm trying to get my life back together. I have to free myself," Eden walks over to me as if he's gliding. He gently takes my hand, putting his hand over mine. The touch of his hand causes my eyelids to blink rapidly. When the movements of my eyelids stop, I am looking through my father's eyes. My out-of-body experience frightens me. I begin to tremble. Eden places his left hand over my head, which calms me. I can see the afflicted standing before my father, crying for help. His heart is heavy. I feel the weight on his shoulders and the absorbing responsibility of saving humanity. There are hundreds of people standing in line awaiting their miracle. The line is becoming disorganized as men, women, children, and the elderly push and shove to get to my father. He stands up, telling the crowd to be patient and he will get to everyone. The people refuse to listen and become more intolerant. A Caucasian male next in line turns to the crowd behind him, demanding everyone listen. The group falls back in line, complying with his instructions for some apparent reason.

My father then proceeds with his healing. He asks the same white male in front of him if he believes Jesus Christ died for his sins. The man answers yes. My father then lays his right hand on the man's chest. He says in the name of Father, Son, and Holy Spirit, healed is your affliction. The man is confused because he doesn't feel anything. He asks my father why he feels the same. My father tells him when he's ready, the miracle will happen. The Caucasian male became irate, asking my father what that meant. He says to my father he's ready right now. How long does he have to wait? My father explained to the man he didn't have faith in God. He says he has to believe entirely, without a doubt. Then, and only then, will he be healed. At this point, the man's face is turning red. He starts yelling insults at my father. He calls my father a phony, a false prophet, and then punches my father in the face, causing him to fall over. A couple of men standing in line grab the white male, tossing him out of the church. I can feel my father's agony, the soreness from the punch against his face, but also the never-ending burden of trying to save souls. Eden again touches my hand, and I return to normal.

"What was the purpose of me seeing this?"

"The man that hit your father is the answer to all your questions."

"I don't understand."

"Search for this man, and then you will understand."

"Eden, I'm a wanted man. I can't just go around asking questions and looking for people."

"Peace, be still!" His baritone voice frightens me. I turn my face away from him.

"Do not be afraid. Stand on your feet. God has selected you to carry out this task. You must comply as written. Paul, you are one of the chosen."

"Are there others like me?"

"There are many others with your ability and some with different gifts. The gift passed down to you and your counterparts is to save the human race from self-destruction. In this day and age, man has forgotten about God. This generation only calls on the lord when trouble is present. When their lives are free from turmoil, they place God on the back burner. A life without God is a difficult way to live. The people of this world call on the lord for prosperity. They cry out to God for money, status, and popularity. If their prayers of fortune are unanswered, they feel God has abandoned them. Their faith is fragile. They call themselves Christians, but when catastrophe strikes, they give up so willingly. God is a loving God, a forgiving God, and a God who never leaves you in times of trouble. He will always find a way out for you when things seem worse. Belief and faith in him are all that's needed. That's where you come in."

"Are you sure?"

"Once again, they need to see what God can do. People have short-term memories. The Lord knows persons believe in him and knows of the sinners disregarding his name. The citizens believing in him need revival. When you display your gift of healing to the kindhearted and worthy, they will give God the glory."

"What if they praise me instead of God?"

"The power you possess works in people with good hearts. They will know your power has come from the lord."

"What if I can't heal some of the sick? Like the man who hit my father?"

"Everyone you touch will have the capacity for healing, but it is up to them to believe. Those who trust in the Lord will receive their blessing."

"What about my faith? How can I heal the sick when my faith is deficient?"

"Paul, I have watched over you for many years. You have been a faithful servant."

"What about my sins? I'm not perfect. The people will laugh at my attempts to heal them. They think I'm a rapist and just recently a murderer who has escaped from an insane asylum. The public will not forget my flaws. God forgives, but people do not."

"God doesn't expect man to be perfect. There would be no need to call on the lord if he were. Trials and tribulations must come for you to seek out God. Give him your burdens, and free your mind of worries."

"I have so many questions, Eden. I just feel inept."

"Paul, you are a great minister. You will be ministering again, but this time with your hands. Preach to the many people you will encounter and then lay your hands on their infirmities. The gift you possess will help strengthen the faith of those seeking out God. Do as I say. God will be with you. I must return now. Carry out your task," the bright light reappears, and Eden vanishes.

CHINA

38

China yearned for affection. Her meager recording sales and Mark's unaffectionate conduct had taken its toll. Jason understands her needs better than anyone else. She looks forward to spilling her heart out to Jason and sharing her many concerns affecting her life. China is a tad bit nervous upon meeting with him. In the years Jason worked for her, she would've never guessed his feelings were this strong. Next to Mark, Jason is short in height and deficient in muscularity. What he lacks in stature, his expertise in the bedroom, makes him productive. Mark is handsome, but Jason isn't chopped liver, either. As China thinks to herself, looks aren't everything. The heart is what matters the most.

With China's mobility hindered, she persuaded Jason to meet her at the mansion. Jason's skepticism made him hesitant at first. After hearing the details of the detectives questioning from China, he's a little apprehensive about meeting her there. He recognizes the police have doubts once she changes her story and places the blame on Mark. He assumes he is safe if she hasn't pressed charges against him. He agreed to meet with her. Over the past seven years of working for China, not in his wildest dreams could he ever have imagined this day would come. She acknowledges him. China conveyed her true feelings to Jason. Mark is a fading memory, a thing of the past. Her interest lies with Jason instead.

Military life had taught Jason to look out for the unexpected. He doesn't believe in coincidences or things occurring out of the clear blue. If something happened, it happened for a reason. Nothing else could explain it. Their relationship is predetermined. It is as simple as that. Jason takes every precaution, traveling en route to China's mansion. He drives around in circles, inspecting his surroundings for followers. When he is positive he's in the clear, Jason heads for China's mansion.

China opens the door with a broad smile, letting Jason inside. He steps inside, staring at her before opening his mouth to speak.

"What I did to you was wrong. It will never happen again. I promise. I lost control of myself. I have a past that has made me this way. I'm not proud of it. I'm trying to change it. I think you're my cure, though," China directs her wheelchair straight for the kitchen.

"I fired my chefs. I fired everyone. I ordered Chinese food. It's on the table. Help yourself. What kind of past are you referring to?" She asks, stopping at the refrigerator to take out a few beverages.

"I wasn't always this bad. At one time, I was a hopeless romantic. I think it started during my youth. I had older parents. My mother gave birth to me at the age of fifty. I'm what you call an old head. My upbringing entailed Sidney Poitier, Bill Cosby, Frank Sinatra, and Fred Aster. Back then, romance was important. Treating a woman like a lady meant everything to a man. Chivalry was alive and flourishing in the world. My male friends called me Mr. Softy, and the girls I encountered over the years weren't any kinder. My gentleman-like qualities rubbed them the wrong way. Instead of appreciating my trustworthiness, they felt it was necessary to do whatever they wanted to me. My kindness became a weakness to them. I cherished the ground they walked on. In return, the women repeatedly used me. I then changed into a different person. I took whatever I needed from them, no questions asked. I became an empty shell of a man. I concentrated on sex and violence. The word love became a bunch of letters without meaning."

"Is that the real reason you turned on me? You told me it was the drinking," she asks awkwardly.

"I would have to say yes. The drinking played a small part. I tried to suppress those feelings, but it hurt me every time you got involved with someone. I visualized us being together and having a family. I was afraid to open up to you. I knew it was next to impossible to become your man.

For one thing, I worked for you. And to top it off, I didn't belong in your league. When you started seeing Mark, I figured I had a chance. He's an ordinary guy like me. The others you dated in the past were filthy rich. The men were more on your level," she is surprised by his response.

"I'm flattered, Jason. Don't take this the wrong way. I don't love you now, but I greatly like you. I thought about you the entire time you were away from me. I craved to be near you, to feel your affection again. I know soon I can grow to love you."

"You think so, China?" He asks, expressing his happiness.

"I know so. That's a fact. You said I'm your cure, right?"

"You most definitely are. You are so beautiful," China is all smiles.

"You still find me beautiful in this big wheelchair?" She hits her hand against the frame. Jason kneels next to China on one knee, comforting her.

"It's only a means of transportation. It can never take away your physical attraction."

"Thanks for sharing that with me. It feels good to hear it," Jason takes a small white box from his pocket.

"Oh my God, Jason, what's this?" China shrieks.

"What does it look like, honey? I've had it for some time," he smiles.

"It looks like an engagement ring," her eyes broaden.

"It can be whatever you want it to be."

"Jason, this is way too fast. We have to go slow, ok. Let's savor every moment together. There's no need to rush it," she said. Her comment was a little disturbing to Jason, but he brushed it off.

"It's just a friendship ring. Go ahead and open the box."

"Are you telling me the truth?"

"Yes, the truth. When our relationship grows deeper, then it can become an engagement ring."

"Ok, I like the sound of that better," China takes the five-carat diamond ring out of the white leather box.

"My God, Jason, how can you afford this?" She asks, examining the ring.

"Don't worry about the money. My love for you is priceless," He takes the ring from her hand and places it on her finger.

"This is so beautiful. I don't know what to say."

"Let me help you then. I know you want us to take it slow. I can respect that. But every time I look at you, you take my breath away. I know all there is to know about you. In the seven years of working for you, I've watched you grow as a person and an artist. You're fun to be around. We make each other laugh. And you're sexy as hell, wheelchair or no wheelchair. I'm in awe of your presence, just like your fans," his generosity touches her. She visualizes the times Mark had abandoned her, several weeks without a single word from him. "Did my comments frighten you?"

"No, not at all."

"You're mighty quiet."

"I was thinking about what you just said. It was very nice," Jason said, standing up and grabbing a beverage from the counter. He untwists the cap off the drink, taking a sip and smiling weakly.

"Nice, that's it? All I get is nice?" She studies him for a moment.

"Let me elaborate some more, honey. It's wonderful. Your words touch me. It's something I haven't heard in a long time. You make me feel wanted again."

"That's much better. For a minute, I wasn't sure if you would respond."

"I've been out of it lately. A lot of changes have happened to me in such a short time. With so much bad news, it's hard to recognize the good."

"You don't have to worry about any bad news from me. It's all good. Do you understand the words that are coming out of my mouth?" She laughs.

"Yes, I do, Chris Tucker. It's one of the things I like so much about you. You know how to cheer me up. Oh, I almost forgot. I have something to show you," China rolls her wheelchair beside the kitchen counter. She takes her hands, lifting one leg at a time onto the floor. Jason tries to assist her. I can do it myself. You don't have to worry," he reluctantly backs away. China then uses her arms to prop herself up. She stands upright for a few seconds before holding the counter for support. "What do you think?"

"I think you will defeat this multiple sclerosis eventually."

"I hope so. It's depressing to live like this. I never thought this would happen to me. My legs are my life. They're part of the reason why I'm famous. I miss dancing. I miss jogging in the mornings. I miss working out with my choreographer. Do you think God is punishing me, Jason?"

"Punishing you for what?"

"I was raised in the church. My mother made sure I never missed a Sunday. She kept me in line, a regular taskmaster. I spent most of my week inside a sanctuary. My friends would come home from school and do their homework, and if time permitted, they would play outside. On the other hand, I had to travel straight to church seven days a week. My mother didn't believe in any time off either. She used to tell me God never takes a day off looking over us, so why should we take a day off from praising his good works? I believe in him with all my heart, and God knows it. I've gotten sidetracked a little, that's all. I think this is my punishment for deserting him."

"China, how can you say this? The entire human race would feel his wrath if this were the case. There aren't any saints walking this earth. You're just experiencing something that has happened to millions of people. Why do you, instead of me, no one knows? But I don't think God himself is singling you out."

"I take it you're right. The cards fall where they choose to fall," Jason says, helping her sit back down.

"Do you still have feelings for Mark?" His inquiry makes her uncomfortable.

"No, honey, I'm only interested in you. Can we not talk about Mark? I want to move forward in my life. Is that ok with you?"

"It's ok with me. I just want to know the truth."

"I'm telling you the truth. Mark and I are not a couple anymore. He kicked me to the curb."

"China, I don't need my heart ripped out of my chest," she sighs.

"There's nothing to worry about, Jason. I'm yours, wheelchair and all. I need to know something as well."

"And what might that be?"

"I need to know if you will ever put your hands on me again."

"I will never put my hands on you again," he tries to sound reassuring.

"Jason, if you're abusive to me, this will never work out. I refuse to live in fear. When a man loves a woman, he's not supposed to hit her. If it ever happens again, I will say goodbye to you forever. I will not allow it," Jason swallows the rest of his beverage. He walks over to the trash can, disposing of the empty bottle of soda.

"Is Mark still in custody?"

"No."

"What do you mean no? I thought you pressed charges against him!"

"Jason, I can't put an innocent man behind bars."

"You just said to me that you don't have any feelings for him," China comprehends the change in his mood. Her fear is beginning to rise.

"I don't, but he didn't rape me. I had to let him go."

"So, I suppose you're gonna turn me in, right?"

"Why would I do such a thing?" His voice gets louder, and his breathing is heavier.

"If he's innocent, then the police will search for me. I'm the prime suspect. Don't you get it? You changed your statement to the doctor, which is incriminating me!"

"Jason, you're scaring me. Please calm down. I didn't tell the police you raped me."

"Oh, so you think there are a bunch of idiots? They're trained detectives. They know bullshit when they hear it, and I know bullshit when I hear it. You still love him. It's why he's free," he looks at her in disgust. "You leave me no choice then."

"What are you saying?" Terror grips her. As soon as her last words leave her mouth, Jason slaps China's face with so much force it ejects her from her wheelchair. She lays on her back, powerless with the air knocked out of her. China tries to catch her breath. It feels like she's slowly fading away. Jason stands over her.

"This is gonna hurt you more than it will hurt me."

DAVID

39

"I know this is tough for you, but can you tell us what happened?"

"He must have followed us from the church, but no one saw him at the funeral services. Everyone attended except him. On our way to my uncle's apartment, Cathy decided to stop the car. She wanted to talk to me. That's when Nate, out of nowhere, opens the car door and grabs her. I think he had a gun pointed at her."

"Are you positive?"

"Yes, because he told Cathy to stay still or he would shoot her. I can't believe he's kidnapped her. He wants to get back at me for being with his ex. She came from Canada to help me. She's done a lot for me. Nate has lost it. You have to find her before he does something terrible."

"The department is on it. We're following every possible lead."

"When I first met Cathy, I misunderstood her. She talked about God a lot. I hated God. When I lost the good things in my life, I figured he didn't exist. How could he exist and let all of these bad things happen to me? But I realized we all have to go through things, big or small. It's just a part of life. I know he's with me because I'm still here kicking and breathing. There's a bullet in my brain, which I can't understand why. I should be dead, but God is keeping me here for something. When I was just a child, my parents died in a car accident. I rode in the same vehicle, and nothing happened to me. Cathy helped me to understand why we are here. I'm here to help others. If everyone could help someone else, the world would have fewer problems. Each one of us has more than enough."

"Do you have any idea where Nate might be?"

"I haven't the slightest clue. After our little fallout when we were teens, we seldom stayed in contact with each other."

"Before the fallout, where did you guys hang out?"

"It was so long ago; we were young. The places wouldn't have any relevance now."

"David, you'd be surprised. People like familiarity. It's what keeps us happy. We hold onto joyful memories and tangible things that make us feel human. There are not many places he can hide. With no money and lack of resources, he won't make it past a week on the run."

"I don't know if this will help, but as a teen, when Nate was feeling down about things, he frequently went to the football field to think."

"A football field?"

"Yes, where I first learned to become a running back. It's where my uncle trained us."

"Where is this field?"

"It's off Springside Avenue near SCSU."

"Is it near the projects?"

"Yes."

"Thanks for your help, David. Your information is important to us. We will get right on it. Is there anything we can do for you?"

"When you find my stepbrother, tell him I forgive and love him. Tell him I'm sorry."

"Ok, will do."

Outside of the police department, the sun is shining brightly. Detective Harry and Kevin put on their sunglasses in a coordinated motion and headed for the unmarked car.

"Kevin, can you believe this week?"

"No, it's like a movie script with plots and twists around every corner, which never seems to end."

"Let me put it in perspective, Kevin. We have a woman, wait, correction, a songstress, when first admitted to the hospital, making accusations her bodyguard raped her. Then, upon our questioning her, she claims her boyfriend did it. She dropped the charges against him a few days later, setting him free. After he's set free, the singer is found in her mansion beaten nearly half to death and is now in a coma."

"How can anyone want to hurt a woman as pretty as her?"

"I don't know, Kevin, I just work here. Then, we have a blind football player who tried to end his life. The gun he used was put there by his stepbrother and traced to a homicide dating back three years. The stepbrother seeks revenge since he believes he lost the love of his life because of the football player. His scorn and jealousy lead him to abduct the football player's girlfriend. Lastly, we have just learned a former pastor who's widely known in the city for his preaching and also for his alleged rape of a church member has escaped from a psychiatric institution accused of killing a patient inside the facility."

"Are you sure there isn't anything else going on today?"

"The day is young. Give it time."

PAUL

40

I have to find out about the man in the vision. I was very young then. His face is unfamiliar to me. My mother would know. I call her from my sister's cell phone. She picks up on the third ring.

"Hello."

"Mom, it's me."

"Lord, you left out of here just in time. The police arrived right after you left. It looked like the entire police force. They asked me if I had seen you. I told them I had not seen you. I dislike not telling the truth. But you're my son, and I hope they believe me."

"If they didn't, you would be in custody right now for abetting a fugitive."

"Paul, I pray to God you get yourself straight. You cannot live like this."

"I know a way out, Mom, but I need your help."

"Paul, did you hear what I just said? The police have been here looking for you, and they will be watching me from now on. If I try to help you, they will know all about it."

"I just have a question for you. Who is the man that punched my father inside the church?"

"How do you know about this?"

"The angel showed me. He said this man is the answer to my questions."

"I'm afraid not, Paul. The man you're looking for is dead."

"Dead, how can that be? The angel told me to look for him."

"Are you certain?"

"Yes, I'm positive."

"The man's name is Benjamin Roberts, Mayor Benjamin Roberts."

"Mayor Benjamin Roberts?"

"Yes, a very crooked mayor, with scandals from here to California."

"Why did he come to my father?"

"He had a rare debilitating disease. It was slowly eating away his body. He asked your father to heal him. Your father gave it his best effort, but the mayor's faith was too weak. He was a mayor of money, not of God. In return, he lambasted your father's works. He formed a commission of crooks to dig up dirt on your father. The commission hit Paul Senior with everything imaginable to bring him down. First, this commission attempted to persuade your dad's congregation not to trust him. When that backfired, the commission investigated his finances, falsely claiming he was profiting off people experiencing poverty. When his records disclosed his finances were in order, they finally decided to kill him."

"The committee murdered him?"

"No one knows the truth, but I know they did it."

"Did the mayor die before they killed my father?"

"Close to it. The Mayor lived quite a while after his diagnosis, but he couldn't get around without a wheelchair or someone looking after him. He looked awful and almost unrecognizable."

"Did the police search for my dad's killer?"

"To this day, I don't believe they have. I believe the killer is still out there. I think the commission hired him. I miss your father. Twenty-five years of marriage taken away from me in a flash."

"Mom, when I find out more information, I will call you back."

"Paul Jr., please be careful. The devil is loose, and he's taking as many souls as he can. Fight him with God."

CHINA

41

When Henrietta heard the news of her daughter being in a coma, she almost fainted. Why China turned away from God was the question she asked herself repeatedly. Throughout China's nurturing, Henrietta read the bible to her. She taught her how to pray, giving China a complete understanding of Christ. China attended Sunday school and bible study. She knows everything about the biblical stories and their meaning. It's hard for Henrietta to look at her daughter in this condition. Henrietta places part of the blame on herself. Her drinking binges before she became saved allowed the devil to get to China. The time she spent getting drunk, she permitted China the opportunity to be influenced by late-night videos. Instead of singing for the lord, China emulated the whoremongers parading around half-naked, chanting their lustful songs. Henrietta's sins from her past have put China in this situation. She gazes at China and is hard-pressed at what she sees. There are deep contusions on her face, lacerations on her arms and legs, and tubes going through her body. Henrietta recognizes whoever did this is the devil himself. She takes out her bible and begins to read the story of Job.

The devil made a wager with God. He understands Job is a faithful servant of the lord. He tells God if calamity confronts Job, he will relinquish his faith. God allows Satan to break his loyal servant. Job suffers immensely from Satan wielding his wickedness. He loses his family and all of his possessions. He also undergoes physical pain, but his faith remains intact. After his trials, God blesses him with more than he could ever imagine. Henrietta identifies her daughter is going through distress that breaks her spirit. She has to search for the lord with all her heart, mind, and soul left. Henrietta kneels and bows her head, calling for the lord to intervene.

DAVID

42

"David, I apologize for my son's actions. My pain is heavy, and my heart goes out to you. He's my only child. Do you know that boy put me through eight hours of labor? I thought I would die giving birth to him, and I feel like I'm dying all over again. His father is a piece of shit. Not once did he ever pick up Nate. His birthdays came and went without even a card from this man. His Christmas presents from Daddy never came through. How can you call yourself a man and forget about your child? Maybe that's where he gets this from his no-good father. I surely didn't teach him how to act this way."

"Keisha, Nate is a grown man. He isn't a child. When we become men, we put away children's things. I appreciate your kind words. What I can't get is when Nate started having this much hatred for me. Keisha walks over to the front door, cracking it open. She glances at the police in front of her apartment, then closes the door, securing both locks.

"Losing Manuela was devastating for him. He would not talk to your uncle and me for a month. He walked around the house like a zombie. It worried me for a while. I didn't know what to do to help him. Your uncle told me not to worry about it and give him time to recover. I waited, and eventually, he came around. But he was never the same to me. When he lost her, he lost part of himself."

"Did she ever try to contact him?"

"You don't remember David?"

"No, I was too busy chasing after girls and doing my football thing. I thought Nate had gotten over her."

"Manuela must have called the house at least a hundred times. Nate would just hang up in her face. He never said two words to her. Until one evening, I think she got tired of him ignoring her. She knocked on the door, and Nate greeted her with rage. He called her a whore and a

73

piece of trash. Nate said she was tainted goods after she let you have a piece of her. Nate told her you've slept with so many girls he wouldn't be surprised if she had a disease. He told her he wouldn't touch her if his life depended on it. I had to hold him back from hurting her. I've never in my life seen him so angry. After that episode, we never heard from her again. Thank God."

"Where do you think he is now?" She looks depleted and utterly exhausted.

"I don't know David. I just hope when the police find him, they don't kill him. He deserves punishment for what he's done. I can visit him in jail. I don't want my son to die."

PAUL

43

"May I speak to Danita Stokes, please?"

"Whom may I ask is calling?"

"It's a private matter. I rather not say my name."

"Just a minute, please," the call is transferred to Danita's office.

"Look, whoever this is, my time is money. I have people to see and places to get to. If you're not one of the persons or places I want to visit, I suggest you hang up now. If you don't have a name, you're unimportant to me. I will give you a few seconds. If I don't like what I hear, the conversation is over. Now speak, starting with your name."

"Wow, you don't waste any time, do you? I guess you're in a hurry to destroy another person's life."

"You have five seconds, "mister, whoever this is," and then the phone goes dead."

"My name is Pastor Paul Mitchell. Do I have your attention now?" Danita attempts to clear her head. Suppose this is Paul Mitchell, who escaped the Bedford Mental Institution along with murdering a patient. Her heart shoots into overdrive from the thought of helping the police catch this rapist aa and now murderer. The story will be an exclusive. She will have her biggest payday yet and a chance to move up the hierarchy of success. Everyone will pursue to hear her story. She envisions the dollar signs. *Oprah, I'm on my way.*

"How do I know this is Paul Mitchell and not some prank?"

"There's only one way to find out."

"And what way is that?"

"Let's meet somewhere."

I'm taking a considerable risk in meeting with Danita Stokes, the reporter responsible for crippling my name. Her chief focus is ratings and money. She believes I raped and beat Patricia Martin. I'm positive she wants me locked away for good, but not without an exclusive interview to show her audience first. Her hunger for stardom will support me in finding the answers I'm looking for. She will use me, and in return, I will use her. Two brains are better than one. Danita can assist in finding out more about this mayor. I need answers fast. My time is running out. I told Danita to meet me at a local McDonalds in the parking lot. I didn't exactly tell her what vehicle I was driving. I informed her to come alone, or everything was off. When she pulls her black Mercedes Benz in the McDonald's parking lot, I wait ten minutes, checking for stragglers before parking across from her and flashing my headlights. She gets out of her car and walks to my sister's vehicle. She opens the door and gets inside.

"Pastor Paul Mitchell, you have a gigantic set of cohunes for someone on the run! What if I'm setting you up? For all you know, this can be a sting operation to bring you to justice," she smirks.

"Danita, I know you better than that. You're here to get some pertinent information to help your career. You need a story; I'm the biggest thing happening now."

"How do you know I need a story?" She looks strange.

"You wouldn't be here if you didn't."

"It had better be good. If it's not, your ass is going to jail. I will make sure of it. I don't trust you. I believe you attacked Patricia Martin and raped her. I should have you arrested. You have nowhere to run."

"Now, think for a minute. Let it sit and marinate. Why would I risk coming to you if I know everyone is looking for me? Does that make any sense, Danita?"

"None of this makes sense to me. What juicy material do you have to share with me?" Her pupils dilate.

"First, I need your help finding out information about a dead person," she looks distraught.

"Are you kidding me? Is this some kind of joke? Do I look like a detective to you?"

"Look, if you get this information, I will give you something significant for me."

"I postponed significant engagements to come over here and meet with you. It seems to me you're pulling my leg. I don't have time to spare. I'm a very busy woman. Why should I help you anyway? The entire state thinks you're criminally insane, not to mention armed and dangerous."

"It doesn't matter what they think. What do you think?" She adjusts her gra,y skirt getting comfortable in the seat.

"I don't know if I can trust you or not."

"Danita, trust me. You won't be disappointed. If I can't give you what you want, I'll turn myself in," she rubs her chin.

"What is it that you want me to do?"

"I want you to look into everything you can about a former mayor of New Haven. He died from a rare disease. His name is Benjamin Roberts. When you find some information on him, get back to me as soon as possible."

"When will I get the information you're promising me?"

"As soon as you can give me what I need."

"I' 'm sorry, Paul, it doesn't work like that. If you want me to work for you, I need security. I need to know whatever information you're holding is genuine. I don't work for free." I must give her something to whet her appetite and keep her digging for information. I reach into the back seat, handing her my father's writings on healing.

"What's this?"

"It's my father's journal on healing," her mouth drops, preceded by mild laughter.

"You have got to be kidding me, right?"

"I don't lie. It's for real."

"You expect me to believe your father healed people?" I nod my head, "Paul, this is crazy, especially coming from an escaped psychiatric patient," she looks at me weirdly.

"I know it's not the norm, but it's true. You have to trust me on this."

"Have you ever seen your father heal anyone?"

"No."

"And you want me to believe this? Let me tell you, I have a career to maintain. If I go on TV claiming your deceased father had healing powers, They'll label me as crazy as this story sounds."

"OK, just read it for me. When you discover what I've asked of you, I will heal someone before you. You can choose the person," she frowns. Her shoulders slump down.

"I knew I was wasting my time coming here. The state put you in an insane asylum for a reason. I think you need to get back there, and I believe it's my job to help the proper authorities put you back inside." She takes her cell phone out of her purse. "I have to make this call. You leave me no choice."

"Can you once in your life help someone other than yourself? Where's your humanity? I came to you because of your reputation for getting the facts right. I'm not crazy. I know what I'm talking about. You have to believe me," she looks into my eyes. The indecision is killing her. She finally decides to place the cell phone back inside her black purse.

"Do you know how this sounds to me?"

"I know it sounds bizarre. All I'm asking for is an opportunity to right the wrongs done to me."

"And you feel this man is the reason for your troubles?"

"I don't know, but it's worth a shot."

"So let me get this straight: if I find what you're looking for, you will heal someone before me?"

"Yes."

"And I get to pick the person?"

"Exactly," she shakes her head in disbelief.

"Have you ever healed anyone before?"

"Yes, it happened when I was a child. I don't remember any of it, though."

"How do you know you did it then?"

"My mother told me I did. When you read my father's journal, you will understand more. It will open your eyes to the truth. This mayor formed a commission hired to kill my father."

"Why would a mayor do such a thing?'

"He was dying, and my father tried to heal him. The healing didn't work because of the mayor's absence of faith."

"So, you're telling me for the healing to occur, he or she must have faith in God?"

"You must accept Jesus died for your sins and believe in the unseen. The healing happened because of their unending devotion. Some in the crowds following Jesus touched his garment and became cured."

"Can I televise this faith-healing thing so the world can see it?"

"I don't have any problems with it. I just need material on the mayor."

"Are you giving me exclusive rights to this?"

"Yes, I am. The world needs to know." Danita's career has been faltering as of late. The prospect of presenting her viewers with a preacher possessing curative powers causes her adrenaline to surge. If this turns out to be accurate, she will show this in the homes of the American people. Everyone around the world will know her name.

"I'll do this for you," she says tentatively. "I can't believe I'm about to help a rapist."

"Look, I'm not a rapist. She framed me. The truth will come out. Just get the information I need."

CHINA

44

Henrietta's prayer is interrupted after a knock on the door. She kindly tells the person at the entrance to come in. Mark walks inside the room. Henrietta cracks a light smile.

"It was nice of you to come."

"I thought about not coming. China had me arrested. It hurt. I almost lost my job behind it. But then I realized I hurt her as well. I wasn't there for her when she needed me the most. No matter what she did to me, I can forgive her. She's a sweet person deep down inside."

"Who did this to her?"

"Her bodyguard."

"Jason?"

"Yes."

"He's been working for China for years. Why would he do this?"

"He has a history of abusing women. He's done something like this before."

"Why isn't he in jail then?"

"The women he physically assaulted were too afraid to testify against him. Plus, he had an excellent lawyer."

"Our legal system is terrible. Instead of punishing criminals, it protects them."

"What did the doctor say concerning China's health?"

"She said China has a 50-50 chance of coming out of this coma. It's my fault, Mark. I could have been a better parent to her. I allowed her to go astray and away from the lord," she wipes her eyes.

"It's not your fault. Don't blame yourself. You raised China the best way you could as a single parent. She turned out to be a wonderful person. I was amazed at how she touched her fans when I watched some of her concerts. It was as if she was a God to them. I saw some of them cry, scream, and fall out from hearing her sing. She affected her audience in ways we can't understand. She has a gift, Ms. Reynolds. I know you want her to use her gift for the lord, and we discussed it a lot. I believe she did use her gift for the lord."

"You do?"

"Have you ever listened to any of her music?"

"No, I only listen to Christian music. Secular music is lust, temptation, and everything else that can cloud your mind."

"Some nonspiritual songs aren't all bad, Ms. Reynolds. For one thing, China's music is uplifting. Her songs carry a positive message throughout. Her lyrics cater to women from all walks of life. She's their voice of reason. I've listened to most of her songs, and I can tell you there's nothing derogatory in her lyrics. China sings about empowerment. She hasn't forgotten what you taught her. Her music is not as Christian music, but it's close to it."

"I never knew this. I just assumed China was singing the devil's music. I am wrong for thinking this about my child. I feel ashamed. I never gave her a chance to explain to me honestly. I misjudged her. Yea, shall judge not saith the lord. Do you pray, Mark?"

"Sometimes, not like I should. My mother and father are Christians, and I am baptized."

"Well then, give me your hand," Mark sticks out his hand. She grabs his hand and instructs him to kneel at the foot of the bed. "Mark, bow your head and close your eyes. God will hear us together."

"Ok," Henrietta begins to pray.

"Dear omnipotent lord of lord and king of kings. We come to you as humble servants asking for your generous sanctification. We come to you in need of a miracle. Lord, I know it's a miracle just to be alive, to have food on our table, to have a job to pay our bills, and to have a roof over our heads to sleep comfortably at night. Lord, forgive us for our sins and wrongdoings we sometimes indulge in. Help us to stay connected to your light that never dies. Help us to remain faithful servants amid trouble. Help us to be more charitable to others in need. Help us to understand our greater cause as human beings. Teach us to be better servants of Christ. Gracious God, my daughter is in trouble. Her life is in chaos. Her predicament is desolate. The doctor says she has a 50-50 chance of coming out of her coma. Lord, but I believe you have the final say overall. You made the doctors who issue the prognosis. You made the medicine that relieves our pain. You carry us when we are incapable of carrying ourselves. Lord, in the name of Jesus, touch her infirmities and make her whole again. Please have mercy on her soul and give her a second chance at life. If it's your will, lord, let your will be done. Amen."

DAVID

45

"What will you do now, David? Are you going back to Canada or staying here in CT?"

"I will probably stay here in CT. If Nate gives up Cathy, and I believe he will, I can convince her to stay with me."

"You will?" Keisha asks with absolute exhilaration. "I pray to God he does. I don't even know my son anymore. He's a total stranger to me," her exhilaration fizzles.

"He will come through. It's not in his character."

"I hope you're right."

"There's nothing left for me in Canada. My football career is over, and I don't have any family there. You're all I have left. I appreciate everything you've done for me. I figure we can help each other."

"David, don't make me cry. I've been crying for what seems like an eternity this past week. So much pain has happened."

"Keisha, I was thinking about opening up a haven for troubled youth in the city," she raises an eyebrow.

"Do you think this is a good thing?"

"Why wouldn't it be?"

"For one, the kids in this city will shoot you over a dollar. Two, they don't have any respect for adults. And three, it's hard to bond with them. I'm not trying to steer you away from helping; I'm just warning you it won't be easy."

"I realize it won't be easy, but my challenges are much worse than a bunch of unruly teens."

"What happens when your sight returns? Will you continue to play football professionally?"

"It's going on two months, Keisha, and I still can't see a thing. To tell you the truth, I haven't been focusing on my sight. I'm kind of getting used to it. I see what I can't see in the day at night in my dreams."

"What kind of dreams?"

"I see everyone. I dream of my mother, father, Uncle Chuck, and grandmother. It's kind of weird, but they talk and advise me. It's the strangest thing. It feels like I never lost them. When I visualize my family in dreams, their skin is perfect, and everyone looks young again."

"You know David, people say when loved ones pass over, we see them happy in our dreams. Their uncertainties, diseases, and pain and suffering are no more. What kind of advice are they giving to you in your dreams?"

"On more than one occasion, I heard them say that God will restore my sight in his time, not mine. They often tell me to be patient."

"Well, David, there you have it. Do you believe in their words?"

"I didn't at first, but now I'm starting to believe it. I can almost sense it. Cathy's made a big impression on my life. I promised her I would strengthen my faith in God. I told her I would pray more and attend service regularly. I made a promise to her, and I will keep it."

"You can attend the church I go to, David. It's not that big. It's where your uncle and I went most of the time. The members are amiable. The choir is awesome, and the pastor brings the fire to the pulpit. I think you will enjoy it. New members are joining all the time."

"That sounds good to me. I have to start somewhere."

PAUL

46

I sense a change coming, the transformation from accuser to victim. Danita Stokes is excellent. Perhaps even the best when it comes to discovering facts. In a short time, she gave me what I needed. When I read her report, I was surprised to find the former mayor involved in so much illegal activity. The feds accused him of stealing money from the treasury to support his gambling habit and drug addiction. He owed thousands in back taxes. His home was in foreclosure, and his wife filed for a divorce because of his infidelity. He accepted corporate kickbacks, allowing them to dump contaminated waste into the Quinnipiac River. He gave away civil service jobs to outside residents less qualified than the ones living in New Haven. There wasn't much information about the commission that killed my father. Their names were undisclosed, but there was information leading to a woman, one of the Mayor's many indiscretions costing him his marriage. Danita said she lives in the city. Last night, I slept at a truck stop outside the city limits in my sister's vehicle. She worries about my safety. I told her I was onto something that might help my situation. I slept pretty well. I start the car, heading for the mayor's former mistress. The address Danita gave to me is a local daycare. She said the woman works there as a childcare provider. A childcare provider and a crooked mayor don't seem to match. Nowadays, anything is possible.

Danita informed the woman she was running a story and needed to interview her about the former mayor's past dealings. She told her I would meet her in the parking lot and jot down some notes. The interview would take no more than twenty minutes of her time. She agreed. The small structure sits in the center of apartment buildings, a convenience store, and Salim's pawn shop on Dixwell Avenue. I turn off the main avenue into a narrow driveway while checking my surroundings periodically for unwanted company. At the end of the driveway, I squeeze my sister's SUV into a miniature parking space where a woman stands alone. She's an older woman, I'd say in her sixties. Her salt and peppered hair is cut short. She's wearing a white and black multilayered dress. I roll down the window, telling her I was sent here by Danita Stokes to interview her. She gingerly walked over to my window, giving me a thorough inspection.

"I don't get into cars with strangers. If you want this interview to happen, it must happen with me standing by your window."

"Mam, it's not a problem. Whatever works for you?"

"I'm not trying to insinuate you're a bad person, but you never know these days. You can never be too cautious."

"I approve. The world is full of shady people," she looks familiar. I know I've seen her before, but where?"

"My break is only a half-hour long. I have to get back to my little angels. I love working with children. What would you like to ask me?"

"Did the mayor have a commission working for him?"

"Yes."

"Do you know their names?"

"I never knew their names. I know they existed, though. When the Mayor got into trouble, the commission cleaned up his mess. They were like an eraser, wiping his slate clean. He paid them very well."

"Can you remember any of the jobs this commission performed for the mayor?"

"I can only remember one job specifically," she says, lowering her brown eyes.

"Did it involve someone getting killed?" She takes a step back from the window.

"Octavia."

"Octavia?"

"It's my name. You don't have to call me mam. I'm a little weary when it comes to bringing up the past. The only reason I'm doing this is because I promised Ms. Stokes. I like her a lot. She looks out for her people. The commission helped me and my daughter."

"How?"

"It's a long story, but I will make it quick," she looks at her watch. "The commission saved me from doing jail time. Before I became this wholesome-looking woman standing in front of you, I was a prostitute. A life I wish I could forget. I ran away from home in my teens. I roamed the streets thinking I was old enough to take care of myself. I slept on park benches. I shoplifted and stole things to survive in the streets. It wasn't long after that when I met a pimp. He took me in. I was just a child. He promised me the world, and of course, I believed him. What child wouldn't? He had money, good looks, and a charming way of talking to you. His words always sounded perfect and touched my heart. He knew how to light my fire. I was a virgin. He had me wide open for the taking. He showered me with gifts and put me in my apartment. I thought life couldn't get any better than that. That's when my fairytale ended. He introduced me to the devil living inside of him. He forced me to give up my body to men. He made lots of money as I lay on my back. He pimped me out to doctors, lawyers, teachers, and a politician, one in particular."

"The mayor?"

"Yes. The mayor became my favorite client. I saw something in him that made me fall in love with him. I even let myself get pregnant by him. I thought by having his child, he would free me from the pimp, but he shattered my hopes when he didn't want me anymore. I was good enough for him to sleep with me but not enough to bring me home to his family."

"What about your child?"

"I had to raise her alone. The mayor refused to accept her."

"Did the pimp help you raise her?"

"No. The mayor was enraged when I became pregnant. It cost him money. He denied having anything to do with her. After she was born, he beat me constantly, reminding me of the money he'd lost."

"I'm so sorry."

"Don't be sorry. It was years ago. I'm a new person now. I'm a saved woman. The blood of Jesus saved me."

"You said a death occurred?"

"The commission saved my daughter and me when after the pimp died in my apartment."

"The commission killed the pimp?"

"No, my daughter did."

"How?"

"She stabbed him to death."

"How old was she?"

"She was ten years old at the time of his death. I panicked. I didn't have anyone to help me except the mayor. He contacted his commission, and they fixed it. When he first saw his daughter, he fell in love with her. He took her away from me. He said she was better off with him and would have a greater chance of surviving and becoming something more. I didn't argue with him. I was fairly young. I wanted my freedom. It was the worst mistake I ever made in my life."

"Did your daughter stay in contact with you?"

"Initially, she always called me and spent the weekends with me. As she got older, she rejected me. The mayor put her in the best schools. He surrounded her with people with the same interests she had. His new wife couldn't have children, so my daughter made her feel like a parent. His wife introduced her to beauty pageants and modeling. My daughter can attract attention from anywhere. She is beautiful, but she has a flaw. She has an evil side to her. After she killed the pimp, she became something different. It's like her action in taking the life of the pimp turned her into a monster. She can be the sweetest woman, but don't stir her wrong. She'll make you pay for it. Well, I hope this information has helped you. I have to get back. I want to eat something before returning to the classroom."

"One more question: what's your daughter's name?"

"It's Patricia. Patricia Martin."

"I knew your eyes looked familiar. Your daughter has your face."

"Do you know my daughter?"

"Yes, very well," I try to conceal my pain.

"Did she hurt you?"

"She hurt me pretty bad."

"Why?"

"I don't know. I've been trying to figure it out."

"You look familiar, too. Wait a minute, I know who you are. You're the pastor accused of raping her, aren't you?"

"Yes, but I didn't rape her. I still love her. She's all I think about. It's hard to get her out of my thoughts. I'm trying to understand, but I can't figure it out. Why would she frame me and put me through all of this?"

"The only reason I believe your words is because you have life remaining in your body. If you had hurt her in any physical manner, you wouldn't be here to tell it. Patricia would have taken care of you a long time ago. She doesn't forgive and never forgets. Many of her so-called girlfriends over the years can testify to this. She has put many of them through hell. She's hell on wheels. I suggest you stay away from her if you want to live."

"I can't, Octavia. I have to find out why," she shakes her head.

"You've done something to her. How are you connected to the mayor?"

"He came to see my father when he was sick. Oh my God. Now I know. Thank you, Octavia. Thanks for your help," she said, staring at me.

"Son, before you take on this task of finding my daughter, you will need some help. Trying to catch Patricia alone is suicide. I get off at five, come back then. I might be able to help you."

CHINA

47

The sting operation is in motion. Detective Harry and Detective Kevin used every available resource to apprehend their suspect. Finding Jason appeared to be a daunting task until Detective Harry checked his files for a second time. Inside the files were photos of the previous women he assaulted. Each one was similar to the other in hair color, eye color, and body type. Jason preferred a select group of females. This information was essential in apprehending him. The detectives then acquired the services of a female detective disguised to play the role of the victim. Getting Jason to chase after the bait took some thought and preparation. Also in the files were details from his accusers of the locations he spent time at the most. Victim number one stated she met him at a local strip joint in Sumter, South Carolina. Victim number two stated she met him inside a mall in Canton, New Jersey, and victim number three said she met him in Baltimore, Maryland, at the Harbor Fest. Detective Harry chose the furthest location from CT.

It was a lead, but a very small one. The detective trusted Jason would be there looking for his next victim. Detective Harry contacted the South Carolina Police Department, the New Jersey police department, and the Maryland police department, sending each department a picture of Jason. When he turned up in South Carolina, the proper contacts notified him. With the assistance of the South Carolina police department, the sting operation is in motion. The strip club is on an old sanded white creek road with large pine trees adjacent to a swamp. The hot and muggy weather draws a cast of fog around the club. The limited visibility makes it convenient for the police not to be recognized in their unmarked cars. A total of four vehicles border the perimeter. On high alert, each undercover officer has a picture of Jason. The rear and front doors are covered, as well as the roof. No sooner than Jason enters the club, the female undercover officer walks in behind him disguised as his previous victims. She sits next to him at the bar, ordering herself a beer. He takes a long, lustrous stare at her and strikes up a conversation.

"Hi, I'm Felix," he puts out his hand. She shakes it.

"Hi, I'm Dory," she says, stretching her southern vernacular.

"Do you work here?" He moves closer to her.

"Do I look that obvious?" She smiles.

"I suppose. Most women usually avoid this place unless they are lesbians, and you don't look like you're gay to me."

"No, I'm strictly dickly, I don't do the woman thing. I'm new here, but I've been dancing for a minute."

"How come I've never seen you before? I know most of the girls here," she thinks of something substantial to say.

"Are you from here?" He cautiously surveys her.

"No, but I visit from time to time."

"That's probably it, then. You haven't been here long enough to notice me. Remember, I just started," Jason thinks it over.

"I guess you're right because I would remember from the looks of things."

"Will you stay to watch my performance?"

"Most definitely, how can I not," he licks his lips.

"Are you a big tipper? Can you make it rain?" He watches her slow, sultry walk to the stage.

"Show me what you got, and you'll see for yourself," he smiles.

"Are you sure you can handle all of this?" She smacks her rear.

"It's only one way to find out. Let me take you home after your performance," she gives him a satisfied expression.

"We shall see handsome. My girlfriend usually takes me home."

"I guess you must tell her you already have a ride home tonight."

"I have to think about it. You might be a lunatic for all I know. If I let every man take me home who asks me, what kind of woman would I be?" He looks at her oddly.

"I tell you what, we can go outside after my show and chat a little more. How does that sound to you?"

"It sounds good. I like it." She disappears behind the stage and returns in a few minutes. He looks confused.

"What happened? Aren't you performing?"

"I forgot there's another dancer before me. I'm next. What about that talk?"

"You lead the way, ladies, first." When the female undercover officer leaves the strip club with Jason following behind her, he is knocked to the ground by four detectives and handcuffed.

DAVID

48

"I love you, Angie."

"You don't love me, Nate. I'm convenient for you. You live off my disability. You never search for a real job because my money covers most of our bills. You only stay with me because you feel sorry for me."

"That's not true. I love you!"

"Just stop it, Nate. Just stop saying it because you don't mean it. Manuela was the only person you ever loved, and you know I'm telling the truth. That's why you kidnapped that woman, isn't it? You had to get back at your stepbrother for losing Manuela. Just face it, Nate, you've never gotten over her. I hear her name on your lips night after night in your sleep. Sometimes, it awakens me, and I just sit there listening to you talk to her in your dreams. For three years, you've been calling her name. I feel sorry for you, Nate. I love you, but you don't love me. You never have."

"Angie, I have nowhere to go. There are cops on every corner. I'm so afraid. I've never been to jail before. I don't want to die in jail," he cries.

"Nate, listen to me. You're not a bad man. You just made some bad decisions from being hurt. The anger made you do it. Why don't you just turn yourself in instead of taking the risk of being killed by the police? You can get a lawyer to help your case; I have a good one in mind. I have one right next to me as we speak. All you have to do is to turn yourself in."

"I don't need a lawyer because I'm not going to jail."

"Let's be reasonable, Nate. If you turn yourself in now, we can plea bargain for a lesser sentence. How does that sound?"

"Who is this?"

"I'm a lawyer to represent your case."

"I don't need a lawyer."

"Nate, yes, you do. I'm sorry for what happened years ago. I didn't mean to hurt you."

"Manuela?"

"Yes, Nate, it's me."

"I thought you wanted to be a doctor?"

"I thought so, too, but sometimes life takes you down a different path. I'm here to help you. I will represent you if you let me."

"Did you ever get married, Manuela?"

"I did for five years, and then we grew apart."

"Do you have children?"

"I have a son. His name is Nate."

"His name is Nate?"

"I named him after you. Will you turn yourself in and let Cathy go free for me?" Nate doesn't give it a second thought.

"Yes, Manuela, I will turn myself in and let her go," Detective Harry shakes Manuela's hand as they leave Nate's apartment.

Chapter 49

"Patricia Martin killed my father seeking revenge for her dad. She believes my father failed the former mayor. But in truth, his lack of faith failed him. My father did everything possible to help the mayor's condition. I'm confident when the mayor died, she came after my father and shot him. She made it look like an attempted robbery. I was eighteen years old when it happened. He died on my birthday. I also firmly believe she broke into the Psychiatric facility, killing Alexandria to frame me. Her vengeance has no end. For Patricia to hold onto this kind of rage is scary. I guess killing my dad wasn't enough for her. She focused on me as well."

"Paul, you're his son and will inherit your father's legacy. She wants his name erased. You represent him, and you favor him entirely. What's your next move?"

"Danita, I don't know. Her mother is willing to help me, but how can I prove she did all these things?"

"With my help, but first, you have some healing to do. Remember?"

"I remember. Do you have a person in mind?"

"I have two people."

"Danita, all I can say is I hope their faith in God is for real. If not, it won't matter what I do. They must truly believe in Christ and that he died for our sins. There isn't any other way. Are they Christians?"

"I have no idea, Paul."

"What are their names?"

"David Parks and China Reynolds."

"The two you reported on at the hospital?"

"Yes."

"Where are they now?"

"China remains in a coma at the hospital. David is staying with his stepmother. I think it's safer for you if we try David first."

"I agree. I cannot risk getting recognized."

We arrive at the apartment where David is staying. Danita sets up the camera equipment, preparing the living room for her anticipated event. Keisha is very nervous, and David doesn't know what to expect from me. It's been a long time since he's seen anything. When Danita phoned him and Keisha about his chances of being cured, he seemed convinced. David heard the reports along with everyone else on how I raped and beat a member of my congregation. He knew I escaped from a mental asylum along with being accused of murdering a woman inside the facility. I told him not to focus on my shortcomings but to put his trust in God. I ask David to believe he's healed, and it shall come to pass. The sound of my voice reassures him. My words comfort him. He looks overjoyed and ready to be cured of his afflictions. David stands in front of the camera. I stand alongside him with my hand over his eyes.

"David, do you believe Jesus Christ of Nazareth died for your sins?"

"I do believe this."

"Do you believe God gave the world his only begotten son to save us?"

"I do believe this."

"Do you believe in one God and one God only?"

"I do believe this."

"In the name of the Father, the Son, and the Holy Spirit, you are cleansed of your afflictions. The blood of the lamb saves you. Your faith in God has cured you. Open your eyes, David, and see once again," he says, using his fingers to remove the cloud of film attached to his eyes. His eyesight adjusts to the things around him. Out of his peripheral vision is the image of Keisha crying before him. He can visualize the camera and Danita standing dead center in the living room.

"I can see! Keisha, I can see again," he touches his eyes. "Oh my God, I can see! It's a miracle. I have feelings in my hands. Everything is back to normal. Pastor, I owe you my life."

"You don't owe me anything. You owe God everything. Use your knowledge and renewed faith to help someone. Carry out his mission. Give to those in need. Help people experiencing homelessness and take care of the orphans. Our job on earth is to serve. It's not to glorify ourselves. God be with you on your journey."

Danita Stokes is speechless for nearly ten minutes. The sight of David's healing is astonishing to her. She checks the camera to make sure it has recorded everything. When the footage is suitable, she packs up the equipment.

"Paul, what just happened in there? I don't know what to say. I've never seen anything close to this in my life. I have to admit I doubted your ability. Deep down in my heart, I knew there was no way you could heal this man. I'm not very religious. I attend a catholic church once a month if I'm lucky. I can't wrap my brain around what you just did. It's not supposed to happen."

"Why isn't it?" She folds her arms and appears to be trembling.

"You're just a man, that's why," she tears. I rub her shoulders, consoling her.

"Danita, God created man in his image. Why is it hard to believe God lives in us and easier to believe in satanic powers?"

"I can't answer that."

"The problem with the human race has to do with our faith. Miracles are happening all around us every day. Not just the miracle of giving sight to people who are blind but the miracle of cancer vanishing from a person diagnosed with a month to live. What about the phenomenon of a physically abused child growing into a caring and loving parent or a person escaping a near-death experience? The earth is full of miracles. To witness another day is a miracle. Nothing's promised. We accept bad things and look for the worst. Why do you think evil is so pervasive?"

"We believe in it?"

"Correct, we breathe life into the bad things. We open the door for Satan when we give up hope and shut out God in the process. The devil can only get to us if we allow him. The choice is ours. The devil is a lie."

"Paul, will you be able to heal China Reynolds just like you did here?"

"Yes, but how will I get to her without someone seeing me?"

"Let me handle it. You just take care of your healing powers."

Before we formulated our plan, Danita made contact with Henrietta Reynolds. She spoke to her about our proposal to save China's life. Henrietta was confident I could do what Danita told her over the phone. She knew about my father's healing ability years before. She said he was a great man and gave so much of his life to saving people. Henrietta declared God answered her prayers when Danita's phone call came through. She started to speak in tongues during their conversation. After Danita talked to Henrietta, we made our way to the hospital. Walking up to the reception desk at the hospital gives me the jitters. I keep adjusting my brown afro wig and artificial mustache.

The wide-rimmed glasses I'm wearing keep sliding down my nose. My disguise looked hideous, but Danita intended to get me inside undetected.

Danita is wearing a shoulder-length black wig with brown highlights. I have a beige polyester suit, and Danita is sporting a floral sun dress. Our hands are intertwined as we approach the desk as a married couple. To any onlookers, we are definitely from the seventies era. Danita gives the albino female receptionist China's last name. She gives us an in-depth inspection as she can see through our ugly disguises.

"How may I ask, are you related to the patient?"

"We're family. I'm her first cousin on our mother's side, and this is my husband. Can't you see the resemblance?" Danita asks. The receptionist gives us an unsettling look.

"I'm sorry, mam, but I don't see it."

"Are you trying to insinuate that's not my cousin in there?"

"Mam, I'm not suggesting anything. I have to follow the procedure. China is not your regular patient. We have to protect her as best as we can. What is your name?"

"It's Mr. and Mrs. Daniels."

"Hold on a minute. I need to confirm it. I have a Mr. and Mrs. Daniels to see China. Um, hum, are you sure? Ok then, I got it. I'll send them right up. Everything checks out. You can go up now. It's room 312. I'm sorry for your inconvenience. We just have to make sure."

"No problem, honeybun. My husband and I understand. You're doing a fine job protecting our China, and you do it very well. Have a good evening."

"Danita, if this reporter thing ever fails you, you would make an excellent actress.

"Please, I'm no Halle Berry."

"But you're pretty good," she laughs at my compliment.

"Ok, whatever you say."

Not every day you get an opportunity to come face to face with a real-life celebrity. Today is my day, but I wish the terms differed for both of us. I've heard her songs and seen several of her music videos. I think she's an outstanding singer. She has a voice identical to none. China has thousands of fans here in the US and many more globally. Seeing her in this condition is disheartening, but with God's incredible power, I'm here to change her circumstances. Her mother greets us at the door. She has her bible in her right hand, wearing a silver chain connected to a silver cross. Her long black ruffled dress can pass as a robe.

"Hi, I'm Henrietta, China's mom," she shakes our hands. Her eyelids are moist from crying.

"It's a pleasure to meet you," we say in succession.

"Pastor Paul, you look just like your father, even in costume."

"Thank you. I get that all the time."

"I have a friend that your dad healed. Back then, she had chronic rheumatoid arthritis. She must have seen every physician on the planet and ingested every medicine known to man. As you can imagine, nothing seems to work. The inflammation in her bones and joints hindered her lifestyle. She didn't want to live anymore. Her uncomfortable way of living pushed her to the limit. Many knew your father had healing powers. My friend came to him with her problem, and he cared about it. She has been free of arthritis for twenty years. Your dad had a truly fantastic gift. He sacrificed himself to help people. I respect what you're doing, Pastor Paul. I think it's incredible.

"Thank you. Since China is in a coma, I must ask you a few questions before we begin. Does China believe in God?" Henrietta lowers her head and slumps her shoulders, gazing into the floor.

"Pastor Paul, I raised my baby in the church. She knows all there is to know about the lord. I tried my hardest to convince her to come back to God. She just wouldn't listen to me."

"Is it safe to say China believes in one God and one God only?" She lifts her head, making eye contact.

"Yes, she accepts this," Henrietta nods.

"Does she believe God sent his only begotten son to wash away our sins?"

"Yes, she does," Henrietta affirms again by nodding a second time.

"As long as she believes in God, her complications will disappear. Now, I will begin."

"Do I need to do anything to help?"

"You can pray China receives God's grace," Henrietta responds by kneeling at the foot of the hospital bed. Danita organizes her miniature camera, which she hid from the receptionist inside her handbag. She then starts recording. I walk over to China. I'm very conscientious of her condition. I'm not sure where to place my hand. There are tubes and wires everywhere. I hear the steady pulse of her heartbeat displayed on the monitor. Her face enlarged. There are lacerations covering her cheeks and forehead. I position my hand over hers.

"In the name of the Father, the Son, and the Holy Spirit, you're cleansed of your afflictions. The blood of the lamb saves you. Your faith in God has cured you. The God of Abraham and Isaac have summoned you to wake up from your coma. Rise, I say!"

The metamorphosis of China Reynolds was something spectacular to witness. Not only did her eyes open, and she walked across the floor, but her face returned to its beautiful form, which many of her fans adored. Danita Stokes had her coveted Pulitzer Prize material. She was ecstatic and vowed to help me clear my name of all offenses. Later that evening, I met with Patricia's mother and Danita Stokes again. Danita contacted the two New Haven police detectives who captured China's bodyguard and David Park's stepbrother. She expressed my innocence by letting the officers know Patricia Martin had framed me. She told them to call off the dogs and give us time to prove it, and they would obtain full credit for solving the case. The detectives corresponded with our proposal, agreeing to help capture her. To apprehend a thief, con artist, or rapist, you have to think like one. Those were the specific words coming from Detective Harry. We informed him how Patricia murdered my father along with the killing of Alexandria. Patricia's mother furthermore elaborated on the first time her daughter took someone's life as a child.

I advocated for going in alone. Detective Harry disagreed with my idea of going inside Patricia's home and getting a confession out of her. He suggested it would be beneficial if her mother went in alone wearing a wiretap, bringing her to confess. He stated Patricia would realize something was wrong if I showed up at her door looking for answers as a fugitive and may try to kill me. Octavia agreed to go in alone. She loves her daughter but has disdain toward her for killing an innocent woman. The four of us sit inside a white van approximately four blocks from Patricia's apartment in Stamford, CT—the words Valerie's floral shop is on the van's side door. Octavia is dressed casually in navy blue denim jeans and a long-sleeved blue sweater covered by her black wool coat. The gold pendant around her neck has a wire attached to it, along with a miniature camera inside.

When it was safe to leave the van, she stepped out onto the sidewalk. The one-way residential street is peaceful and consists primarily of two- and three-family homes. Cars sit on both sides of the street, with a few people sitting on their porches. As she gets further away, we can hear her footsteps and visualize the things in front of her through the four closed-circuit televisions inside the van. She sidestepped a few trash cans and climbed the front porch of the brownstone dwelling, ringing the first doorbell. Patricia opens the door, letting her inside. Seeing her through the monitor gives me heartshock. She looks more beautiful than the last time I saw her. My feelings haven't entirely departed. It's been months, but it feels like yesterday. I am a victim scorned by a forbidden love. A love I can never truly have.

"Mother, this is a surprise. What brings you to my neck of the woods? She smiles callously at her mother.

"I thought if I came to see you, it would remind you that you have a mother, remember?" Her mother gives her the same sadistic look in return.

"Oh, how could I ever forget? A child can never forget their mother, especially if their mother is a prostitute. Do you know how difficult it was to live with the thought of men touching you? I had to tolerate it. It was hard for me. I began to hate men. I was unfortunate enough to hear them stick their dicks in you night after night, then dispose of you like trash."

"That was a long time ago! I was young. I made some mistakes I'm not proud of. We all do. No one is perfect, even you," she retaliates. Patricia glares at her.

"Why the hell did you come to my apartment to bring back memories of how you neglected me as a child?" Her mother has just about had enough of her mouth.

"I will not let you stand here and talk to me like this."

"You can always leave and go back to wherever it is you came from," her mother moves closer, waving her finger.

"Patricia, you're not too old for me to slap the taste out of your mouth."

"Mother, you want to go there? You, of all people, know what I'm capable of."

"What are you capable of?" Her mother provokes her more.

"Is this a test, mother? If it is, you will fail."

"Where does this arrogance come from? I carried you in my womb. I gave birth to you. Where is your respect?" Patricia looks at her.

"You may have given birth to me, but my father raised me," the hurt is too much for Octavia to stomach. She contemplates leaving the apartment and takes a step backward.

"That's right, leave. You don't belong here," Octavia looks down at the pendant, remembering her agenda. She brushes off her comment.

"Your father was no better than me. He slept with prostitutes, embezzled money, outsourced jobs keeping minorities underprivileged, and he cheated on his taxes."

"Shut up, he's not here to defend himself! He did everything for me. He sent me to the best schools. He bought my first car and loved me like a real parent. He would still be alive today if that pastor had done his job," she angrily says.

"What, pastor?" She pretends not to know.

"Pastor Paul Mitchell, senior, he pledged to heal my father. It was nothing but a lie. My dad is dead because of him."

"How can you suggest this? It was his time to go. We are all put on timers. When our time is up, we don't have a choice in the matter."

"You don't understand. My father did have a choice, but the pastor chose not to help him. He healed everyone else except my father. I had to make him pay."

"Did you kill him, Patricia? I hope to God you did not."

"What do you think mother?" She devilishly grins.

"You killed him because your father died?"

"I sure as hell did. I shot him to death. It was simple and very satisfying. But afterward, a hole in my heart remained. My anger wouldn't subside. I needed more."

"What are you talking about?" Octavia looks at her strangely.

"The need for revenge persisted. I channeled all my rage to Paul Jr. How fitting, I thought, to see another pastor marching around as a savior with the same inherited bloodline. I made him fall in love with me. It was so easy. I managed to divert him away from the pulpit and his God. I framed him. I got him arrested. And now, as we speak, he is on the run for his life. I think my revenge is complete," she laughs. Her confession sickens Octavia.

"He's accused of murdering a patient. Was that your work also?" Octavia is afraid to hear the answer. Patricia forms a satisfying smile.

"That, I have to admit, was some of my best work. I walked right into the facility unnoticed. It was a piece of cake smothering that woman and placing Paul's clothes on the scene. I would love to see his pitiful face when they issue him the death penalty. His father's legacy will be no more. It ends with his son. My dad will be able to mourn in peace."

I listen and watch the monitor in disbelief. Patricia is a cold-blooded monster. I never saw her coming. She blindsided me with her beauty. I fell for her lies. She killed my father and etched out Alexandria. How many more people has she murdered? Her vengeance has no end. It's terrifying to imagine anyone with this amount of rage inside of them, but to have fallen in love with one is even more frightening. The two detectives have heard enough to arrest her on the admission of her crimes. The detectives leave the van with Danita Stokes and her camera crew close on their heels. I stay inside, watching the monitor and staring at her appearance for the last time.

Epilogue

Inside the Channel Eight news studio dressing room, the makeup artists and lighting crew prime their guests for Danita's live interview. David and China sit patiently as their faces are dabbed and powdered in cosmetics. The important footage of their healing aired fifteen minutes prior. The time has come to share their experiences with the world. On cue, Danita presents them to her viewers at home.

"America, allow me to introduce the two persons healed in the video. On the right of me, and I'm sure she needs no introduction, is the beautiful singer and songwriter China Reynolds. And sitting next to her is Mr. Football himself, David Parks. China and David, I must say, after seeing the video, I'm still at a loss for words. Can you tell the viewers what was happening inside you during your healing?"

"It's difficult to explain. If you can take every happy moment in your life, put it in a glass, and consume it, I think that describes it best. It's happiness at full throttle. Every negative thought, bad experience, failed opportunity, and fear disappeared. The feeling was wonderful, true bliss."

"Thanks for sharing your experience with us, China. Mr. Parks, can you also elaborate on your experience?"

"It captured the true essence of life. God created us with love. He sketched us in his image. Hate, envy, dishonesty, greed, jealousy, and lust are not part of God but of man. God himself is the highest form of love. He is true goodness. When touched by God, all other things in life fall beneath you. Obstacles and limitations are no more."

"Thanks for sharing with us, David. China, will you continue your singing career?"

"I will. Singing is my life, but I will sing for the lord. I'm working on a new gospel CD. The release is in six months. My new focus in life is to inspire others to gain an understanding of God. God has a purpose for us all. Whatever your God-given talent is, use it, don't waste it."

"Mr. Parks, will you resume playing football?"

"I will not. I'm using my speed and quickness in a different arena. I will run the race God has set before us, the race to help those who can't help themselves. I'm in the process of building a few group homes for troubled males. I will need the help of anyone who can volunteer their time. Our young black men are crying out for help. When will we hear them?"

"Mr. Parks, I commend your efforts and put me down as a volunteer."

"I can help too," China says.

"Well, my faithful, there you have it. My guests today have earned a second chance in their lives, a second chance to make a difference. When will you make yours? Pastor Paul Mitchell, wherever you are, thank you kindly for allowing me to air your story to the world. You've made me a believer."

After healing my first two individuals, I returned to my father's old church building. The vivid memories of his preaching are more vital than ever before. I can see him putting his hands over the sick and afflicted as crowds cry out to him. My father was a fantastic man. He never complained of what God called him to do. He sacrificed his life to give a person a second chance at living. I think long and hard about what I'm capable of achieving. I can save so many people and open their eyes to the meaning of life. I accept my task with enthusiasm. I will not disappoint my father; better yet, I will obey the lord. Amen.

THE END